SERVED COI

Book two Series Four
John Gammon Peak District
Detective books from the award-winning author Colin J Galtrey.

Detective Inspector Gammon is
not your usual detective. He was
a high-flying detective in
London until he received the call
to help find a serial killer in the
beautiful Peak District of
Derbyshire in Book one Series
One "Things will never be the
same again"
This appealed to John he still
had family and the Peak District
was his former home.

The books have created a life of
their own with fans of John
Gammon spending holidays in
the Peak District trying to find
fictional characters that are part

SERVED COLD

of the stories. They almost feel like family members to the readers.

I often receive messages through my web-site www.colingaltrey.co.uk saying that fans have spent short breaks and holidays searching out the fictitious places mentioned such as The Spinning Jenny in Swinster or the Tow'd Man, the Wobbly Man, The Limping Duck and villages such as Hittington, Toad Holes, Swinster, Winksworth Ackbourne and Bixton. We mustn't forget the great walking here in the Peak District through the fictitious Dumpling Dale, Monkdale, Puddle Dale, Clough Dale, Ardwalk and Trissington to name a few.

SERVED COLD

Come with us on this adventure. See how the main characters lives are lived out, the fun, the tragedy, the tears and the friendship that anybody who may have visited the Peak District would be able to associate with.

Hopefully you will find the time to come and visit us. Books in the John Gammon Series in order
1 Things will never be the Same Again
2 Sad Man
3 Joy Follows Sorrow
4 Never Cry on a Bluebell
5 Annie Tanney
6 The Poet and the Calling card
7 Why
8 Your Past is your Future

SERVED COLD

A big thank you for all your support.

To know so many people enjoy and look forward to the next book is very satisfying

Colin J Galtrey

SERVED COLD

SERVED COLD

Chapter 1

It was early March, the fields on the way to Bixton were an absolute delight at this time of year full of spring lambs jumping and kicking. John's mind wandered to the news Saron had told him that he was possibly the father of the baby she was carrying. DI John Gammon was about to have that serenity he felt driving through the Peak District to Bixton shattered.

He arrived at the station in good time this morning aware that some dignitaries from London were visiting and DCI Heather Burns wanted to put on a good show. "Good morning sir". "Yes, good morning PC Magic, all good in the world?" "Not sure sir, I have just sent DI Lee

SERVED COLD

and DS Bass to the derelict
brewery at Winksworth, I had a
call from a Mrs Robins, she is
the care warden at the sheltered
accommodation over the road.
She has reported screaming and
what looked like a man in a
distinctive orange Fiat Panda
rushing from the disused
brewery".

"Probably something and
nothing, let me know if they call
in or when they get back please
Magic". "Will do sir". Gammon
met DCI Burns coming out of
her office. "Good morning
Heather." "Yes, good morning
John". "You look nervous if you
don't mind me saying Heather".
"Hardly slept with this lot
coming from London, these
inspections can make or break
your career" "I don't need an

SERVED COLD

inspection Heather!" and
Gammon laughed. "Do you
want a coffee?" "No thanks
John, just going to speak with
John Walvin and his team before
they arrive at 11.00 am. You
know what they say John "fail to
prepare, prepare to fail" Heather
left Gammon getting his coffee.
Once in his office before he
could tackle his paperwork he
stood with his coffee in his
customary position looking from
his big picture window toward
Losehill thinking what a
splendid day it was. It was now
almost 9.10am and he sat at his
desk when PC Magic rang.
"They have just rung sir, I'm
afraid they have a body". "Ok
get Wally and the team over
immediately and let DCI Burns
know I have gone to the scene".

SERVED COLD

Gammon set off with hopefully a great opportunity to miss the visit. He had never liked them and Heather wasn't wrong, these plastic coppers could ruin a Detective Inspector or a Chief Inspectors career with the stroke of a pen, not that Gammon was bothered, he had up's and down's all his career. Winksworth was an old mining town and had been quite a bustling market town in its day but sadly that was no longer the case. When the brewery shut, the lives of almost a three hundred strong work-force found themselves out of work. Some of the men and women knew nothing else having worked at the brewery straight from school.

SERVED COLD

Gammon pulled into the yard
where, as a kid, all barrels of
beer would be stacked ready for
delivery. Phil, his Dad, would
always insist on a bottle of
Hopton Mild with his Christmas
dinner, he said his dad had
always done the same. Gammon
could see DS Bass talking to a
lady who was possibly in her
early sixties but there was a fair
chance she would be younger.
Fashion appeared to have by-
passed Winksworth over the
years.

Gammon flashed his warrant
card. "Good morning, and you
are?" The lady said "Kathleen
Glossop, I'm the warden at the
old folks place". "So, are you
the lady that called into the
station with the concern?". "Aye
that were me all right". "You

SERVED COLD

say you saw a man leaving the brewery in a distinctive Orange Fiat Panda?" "Yes, our Simon used to have a red un that's how I knew the make" "Simon?" "My son, well he ain't no more, were killed in quarry five year ago" "Oh I am sorry to hear that". "It wanna long after that his dad buggered off" Gammon was wishing he hadn't asked. "Did you get the registration number?" "Of course I did, well part of it UA? 61 ?L?" "Well done Mrs Glossop that's really helpful" "So what were the screams?" "I'm sorry, until we have fully investigated I'm not at liberty to say but we will be in touch and thanks again you have been a great help"

Gammon walked away and headed for Wally and his

SERVED COLD

Forensic tent. "Morning Wally, what delight have we today?" "Woman, possibly mid-twenties, she had a tattoo on her chest and blonde shoulder length hair, slim" "Any sexual interference?" "Give me a break John, I will tell you more tomorrow. Just one thing, on the upper left part of her chest the tattoo was a letter and a series of numbers, the letter A11407 then covered it up with a big waterproof plaster" "How odd Wally" "Yes, now let me get on if you want the info as usual for 9.00am mate". "Thanks Wally". Gammon told DS Bass and DI Stampfer to do a house to house and he would get the traffic lads to lookout for an orange Fiat. He headed back to Bixton and gave DS Yap the Fiats registration to

SERVED COLD

run through the database while
he spoke with DCI Burns.
Magic had told him the visitors
had gone but DCI Burns seemed
upset for some reason. Gammon
climbed the stairs and knocked
before entering her office. Burns
was looking out of the window
when she turned around
Gammon could see she had been
crying. "You ok Heather?"
"Well, sit down John"
"Whatever is a matter? Was it
the visit did it not go well?" "It's
not that John, they are moving
me to Lincoln, they said
Government cuts meant Bixton
was to be downgraded from a
Category B station to C station
which meant we had to lose two
detectives which invariably will
be Stampfer and Finney as they
were the last in I'm afraid and I

SERVED COLD

am to take charge in Lincoln"
"So who is taking on the DCI
role here Heather?" "Nobody,
you are on your own with the
mandate to report to the Chief
Constable if required" "What
about Micklock?" "They are
also under threat". "Bloody hell,
don't they ever learn?"
"Apparently not John" "When is
this happening?" "From today, I
take up my new post in
Lincolnshire with immediate
effect and I have just told Finney
and Stampfer of their fate. I
have cleared my desk, I don't
want any fuss. Good luck John,
you are the best detective I have
had the pleasure to work with"
and she brushed past him with a
small box of her belongings and
she headed down the stairs and

SERVED COLD

out of Bixton. Wow, John thought.

Gammon called a meeting and explained what DCI Burns had said and about DI Finney and DI Stampfer. "We are rowing this boat alone for the foreseeable future". "Sir, how can they cut the station like this when one minute they send people to help us and now they say we need less?" "Good point DS Bass, I don't have an answer but what I do have is still a good team. We have a case currently that I want solving so I expect full support from you all. A woman has lost her life and I intend to find the killer.

Ok Wally what you got for me?" "The woman was in her twenties, we have no dental records on our data base but I do

SERVED COLD

have my team looking further afield. She had beaten with a blunt object maybe a hammer or such like. The next bit is the strange bit, she had the digits A11407 tattooed onto the upper left part of her chest then a large waterproof plaster put over the tattoo. I don't quite understand that, oh and she had some marks on her arms and legs so at some point she had been restrained". "Anything on the plaster or the body Wally?" "Yes, we have loads of DNA but whoever this is isn't showing on our data base" "Is the tattoo new or old?" It looks old but I think it's quite new, maybe just a few days perhaps" "Ok everybody, as this case progresses I want all persons questioned to take a DNA test as a matter of course.

SERVED COLD

Ok everybody let's do the usual house to house and Wally I need this girl identifying as soon as possible please. Thanks everybody"

"Before we go sir, are you now taking control of the station?" "I haven't been officially told Ian but that is what DCI Burns implied and whichever way, it would only be as acting DCI if anything. Ok thanks everybody".

Gammon left the meeting and started on his way upstairs. "I have the Chief Constable on for you sir" "Ok put it through to my office" "Good morning sir" "Good morning DI Gammon, I'm sure today's news came as a bit of a shock but we had no choice, these cuts had to happen. Are you ok with heading up the

SERVED COLD

team?" "Yes sir" "Ok, well I'm not going to disrespect you by calling you acting DCI because that implies a temporary position and from my remit there isn't going to be a DCI in Bixton so that would be pointless and not fair to you, are you still ok with heading up the team?" "To be honest it doesn't sound like there is a choice" "There are always choices DI Gammon, if you don't want the responsibility just say" Gammon could tell he was getting angry so he backed off. "No, that's fine sir" "Ok, periodically I will call you and maybe we will meet a couple of times a year so we can have a chat".

Gammon sat thinking he actually wasn't bothered about the title and he certainly didn't

need the money but he did like
the fact he was running things. It
was almost 3.00pm when Wally
came up to his office. "Hi John,
ok I have a name and a last
known address of our victim".
"Brilliant Wally, go ahead"
"The victim's name is Ruth
Weisner, her last known address
is Apartment three The Lane,
Ackbourne. I believe that is the
old Cotton Mill that was
converted to flats about twenty
year ago, watch yourself if you
are going out there John, it's not
the best neighbourhood in the
world" Gammon laughed
"Thanks for your concern". "Oh,
the tattoo I think was done three
days ago and made to look like
the ones the Nazi's were using
in Auschwitz" "So have we got
a Jewish hater?" "I don't know

SERVED COLD

John but it's certainly sick"
Wally left with Gammon
lamenting over the murder of a
young girl.

Gammon called DS Bass to go
with him to Ackbourne to try
and piece together who Ruth
Weisner really was.
"Congratulation sir" "What for
Kate?" "Your promotion" "I
have been told I am running the
show but there is no promotion"
"To be honest, everybody looks
to you for everything so it's like
you are the boss anyway. I'm
glad I didn't get the chop or
transferred, I have settled in
round here now"
"Well, here we are Kate"
Gammon and Bass arrived at an
old red brick building that was
starting to show its last

SERVED COLD

refurbishment was twenty years
past. Three young lads about
ten-year-old shouted to
Gammon. "Hey mister, do you
want your car looking at? I
could look after your daughter
as well if you want" and the
three of them laughed. Gammon
walked over and showed his
warrant card to the biggest lad.
"Come on, time to go" he said to
his friends. They peddled off
shouting obscenities and
sticking one finger in the air as
they rode away. "Don't think I
ever want kids' sir, not if that is
a sample of the kids today" For
a second Gammon thought of
his own position and Saron's
baby.
The apartment was on the
ground floor, Gammon knocked
on the dingy door, a woman in

SERVED COLD

her mid- thirties came to the door. "Yeah?" she said in a chavvy manner. "I'm DI Gammon and this is DS Bass" and they showed their warrant cards. "You are?" "I'm Tammie Hurts, what do you want?" "We believe Ruth Weisner lived here" "Yeah, there are three of us, me, Ruth when she is here and Susie Carrie. Why what's Ruth done now or is it that waster of a boyfriend?" "Does Ruth have family here?" "Not any more, her grandma passed three week ago" "May we come in?" "Sorry about the mess, we had a bit of a party last night" Gammon could smell the sweet smell of marijuana, he wasn't bothered, that wasn't what he was here for.

SERVED COLD

"I'm afraid Ruth Weisner was found murdered" For some reason Tammie Hurts laughed. "Excuse me, is that funny what I just told you?" "Not funny, bloody hilarious, so the jerk she was with finally succeeded hey?" "What, the boyfriend?" ", Marty Baynes, he is a bloody idiot, we all warned her, he is in to to some heavy shit man" "What do you mean?" "I have said enough, you speak with him" "Where does he live?" "Number Seventeen Dove Crescent, the big council estate in town" "Would you be able to verify the body Miss Hurts?" "Do I get paid?" "No, you are doing it for a friend" Gammon's comment seemed to stop her in her tracks. "Ok, but how do I get there?" "DS Bass. arrange to

SERVED COLD

have Miss Hurts taken to identify the body then taken back here" "Somebody will be here at 11.00 am Miss Hurts. We may need to speak again, good day"

"Blimey sir, she was Miss Personality, what an awful person, how could she laugh at her flat-mates death?" "There is more to this DS Bass, mark my words"
They arrived at the run-down council estate on the outskirts of Ackbourne and found number seventeen Dove Crescent. The garden was overgrown and there was a giant English flag in the bedroom window. DS Bass knocked on the door and a guy with a skinhead haircut, "covered in tattoos and with a swastika

SERVED COLD

tattooed between his eyebrows answered.

"You can piss off if you are stuff" Gammon showed his warrant card. "What now?" "Mr Baynes?" "Yes, what do you want?" "May we come in?" Baynes showed them into the kitchen, tied to the kitchen table was a ferocious looking Alsatian dog. "Don't get too close, he doesn't like establishment people" Bass skirted round the dog that actually looked petrified of Baynes.

"We are here about your girlfriend, she has been murdered" "Really, who would be so stupid to do that?" "What do you mean?" "Well you know who I am, that's why you are here" "We are here to inform you of the death of your

SERVED COLD

girlfriend Mr Baynes" "No you are not, you will try to pin it on me which means you will arrest me then search my house and plant something incriminating like all pigs do" "I can assure you we are not here for any other reason, that aside I would like to know more about Ruth Weisner" "Look man, all I know is she was a sweet girl, we met in the Broken Donkey in Ackbourne three month ago. We slept together, she didn't ask me my business and I didn't ask her business. That's it man, now do you have any other questions because I have a pint with my name on it in the Donkey" "We will probably need to speak again" "Thought as much" Baynes said showing Gammon and Bass out of the door.

SERVED COLD

"Blimey sir, did she have some
nice friends or what?" "When
we get back Kate lets search our
databases for Ruth and Baynes,
let's see if we find anything"
"Ok sir"
Back at the station Gammon
grabbed a coffee and sat
thinking if he should contact
Saron or leave it with her to
contact him. He didn't want her
to be alone with this and if it
was his child he wanted to be
part of its life from the start. He
knew this was like heaven sent if
it was his child, then he had a
family, if it wasn't he wanted
Saron so, if she agreed, he
would bring it up as his own.
He decided to get on with some
paperwork when DS Bass came
into the office. "Not finished yet
sir but this is weird" "What you

SERVED COLD

got so far Kate?" Well, Marty Baynes is a member of HRP 33" "What, the group of skinheads that celebrate Hitler's rise to power in 1933?" "Yes Sir" "Surely with a name like Ruth Weisner she was of Jewish descent?" "So far I have found her family were from Poland and they settled in Ackbourne after the war, not found much else yet sir" "Ok, keep digging please Kate"

Gammon sat doodling with his pen. Why would a member of the HRP 33 group be having a relationship with a Polish girl who was possibly from a Jewish family he pondered? It was almost 6.00pm when he left Bixton and Steve rang. "Hey mate, been ages since we have had a night out. What are you doing Friday?" "Nothing that I can think off" "Ok, I will meet you in the Limping Duck and we can have a pub crawl, India will pick us up at midnight from the Spinning Jenny" "Sounds good to me mate, meet you there, Friday 7.00pm"

John was pleased Steve had been in touch, it seemed ages since he had seen him. He decided to call for a take out from the Spinning Jenny and leave the phone call to Saron for now.

The pub was busy and Kev was in on his own. "Blimey mate, this is an occasion, where's her indoors?" "Oh, some fashion show at Pritwich, she has gone with Sheba, Saron, Cheryl, Rita and Carol Lestar. Think the lads will be in soon. How are you

SERVED COLD

John?" "Yeah ok Kev thanks"
"Pedigree? It would be wrong to
say no" and John laughed. "Pour
one for me and one for John and
we will have a brandy chaser
each please Wez and whatever
you want. Who's the stunning
looking girl with Lindsay Wez?"
It's the sister in law, we call her
Chocolate" "Chocolate, why?"
Well, her names Claire so
Chocolate E- Claire" "Must be
Yorkie humour gone over my
head Wez" "It's an age thing
Kev, dunna worry about it"
Lindsay came over with her
sister. "Hi John, how's life?"
"Pretty good Lindsay" "What
about you Kev?" "Yes good,
loving this retirement thing"
"Wow are you retired, you only
look fifty?" "Well thank you
Claire" "Call me Chocolate,

SERVED COLD

everybody else does. You must be the famous John Gammon" "Not sure on the famous bit Chocolate but I am John Gammon" "You go out with that really pretty girl Saron don't you?" "Careful Chocolate, you are playing with fire" "Give over Kev" "Just warning the pretty girl John that's all" Chocolate laughed showing her immaculate set of white teeth. A couple of drinks later and all the men were in then the girls arrived at almost 10.00pm. At this point John was laughing and joking with Chocolate over by the fire-place, Kev could see both Saron and Sheba were not happy but John by now had drunk too much and was in the don't give a dam mode.

SERVED COLD

The night got so bad that Lindsay asked John if he wanted to stay in one of the guest rooms. Kev leaned towards Doreen and whispered in her ear "Is that a good idea? he is a bit drunk and he has been chatting to Lindsay sister" "You know John Kev, he hits a point a bit like you when he will hit the pillow and be fast asleep. Remember I have put you both to bed many times" Kev smiled "I guess you are right" Around 11.00pm Chocolate made her exit, she could sense the atmosphere coming from Saron and Sheba but most definitely Saron.

Eventually Doreen told Lindsay she and Kevin would put John to bed as he was totally wasted. The following morning

SERVED COLD

Chocolate knocked on his door to say Lindsay had cooked him a full English breakfast, John quickly showered and went out to the dining room. Lindsay had done him proud other than the breakfast was delivered by Wez who painstakingly pointed out what a light weight John was. With the breakfast consumed and Lindsay and Wez thanked John left the Spinning Jenny and headed for work, a full English breakfast always seemed to do the trick. Once at work DS Bass came in his office. "Are you ok sir you look a bit pale?" "Do me a favour Kate, grab me a coffee please?" Kate came back quite excited on what she had found out. "Ruth Weisner had Polish/ Jewish parents, they had both been in concentration camps,

SERVED COLD

David Weisner was captive in Auschwitz and survived, he was liberated and settled in Nottingham, his wife Dora was kept at Auschwitz and also survived ,she settled in Derby but they were reunited in 1948 by the Jewish authorities, they had a son Jacob and he married an English girl Rosie Miller, they had one son born in 1953 and he had a daughter called Ruth, this is our Ruth Sir that was murdered"

"Why would Ruth be with a Nazi sympathiser, it doesn't make sense?" "Maybe she rebelled sir, young girls often do" "Ok, anything on Marty Baynes?" "He is an interesting character, he is thirty -three so quite a bit older than Ruth was and he is a member of HRP33"

SERVED COLD

"Which we already knew Kate"
"Yes Sir but he has also done
time for attempted murder of a
black man in Nottingham, he
was seventeen. Lucky for him
there was an off- duty paramedic
that saved the man's life so he
was only charged with attempted
murder and served fourteen
years and three months, his
lawyer argued at the time that
the black man had hurled abuse
and started it. Because he was
seventeen he will have to report
at regular intervals to the police
for the rest of his life.
Apparently, the witness at the
trial said the black guy started it.
He is now head of HRP 33 and
recruited Baynes" "So how long
as Baynes been out?" "Eight
months sir" "There's still
something not right about this,

SERVED COLD

was Ruth a member of any clubs
or societies?" "Sorry sir, I didn't
look at that" "Take a look Kate,
I am wondering if, for some
reason, he was seeing Ruth more
for what information she might
be able to give"

"Wow sir, I wish I was as good
a detective" "Just experience
Kate, you will get there" Kate
left John working through his
desk full of paperwork, now
Heather had gone he had more
to do.

Kate came back at 4.50pm. "Sir,
it appears Ruth was a member of
the Jewish Survivors Group,
they meet in Ackbourne every
second Friday of each month at
7.30pm at the Town Hall"

"That's tomorrow, Ok, we will
both go and see what this is
about Kate"

SERVED COLD

Gammon left work and decided to ring Saron, it was eating him up not knowing what was what. She answered but sounded really down. "Are you ok?" "Not sleeping John, too much in my head" "Shall I come up straight from here?" "If you want" "Ok, I'm on my way"

Gammon left Bixton and headed to the Tow'd Man, he entered the back way so he could see if Saron was in the kitchen. She was stood prepping ready for the evening meals, John could see she had been crying. "Hey, come on, this should be a happy time" "If this baby was yours John then maybe but I don't know. I have been to the doctor and he said the most positive way is to have either amniocentesis or a chorionic

SERVED COLD

villus sampling, both need a doctor's consent John. He did mention another way which he said he has never used and it's very new to medicine, it is called a NATUS test which can be taken at five weeks, apparently it used to only be done between eleven and eighteen weeks but, either way, I am about twelve I think" "What does it involve?" "Just blood taken from my arm then either a blood sample, hair sample or mouth swab from the man" "Then do it if it means that much to you" "Russell is back in Ireland for a month to six weeks" "Does he know?" "No John, of course not" "So you want it to be mine?" "Well that's a silly question, of course I do, Russell was a drunken mistake"

SERVED COLD

"Forget all that, let's do the test"
"Ok, I will book us in early with
Doctor Tadcastle in Hittington.
Now I'd best get on John, thank
you for being so understanding"
"That's ok" and he kissed her on
her head and left her chopping
cauliflower. John decided to go
straight home, there was a small
fish and chip van that always
parked at Hittington on a
Thursday so he stopped there for
Fish and Chips, Shelley had said
how good they were.
To John's surprise the guy
serving the fish and chips was
Derek Lolly and old schoolmate
John recognised him straight
away he had hardly altered he
was one of those kids that
always looked sixteen and
would be forever being rejected

SERVED COLD

at clubs and pubs when him and
Steve went out as teenagers.
"Bloody hell, John Gammon, I
heard you were back mate".
"Been back a while now, what
about you?" "This is my wife
Molly, we used to live in Crete
until a year ago then Molly had
a few health issues so we came
back and I bought this fish and
chip van" "You doing well
mate?" "Better than we expected
John. What about you?" "Yeah
ok mate" "Sorry to hear about
Adam and your Mum and Dad
mate, are you still married to
Linz?" "No, I'm afraid we split
then she died mate" "Bloody
hell, you have had some trauma.
What about Lineman? I haven't
seen him yet, last I heard he had
fell on his feet and married a

SERVED COLD

lass with a load of money and a looker too I heard"

"I'm afraid she and their daughter died in a fire, Steve is with somebody now though" John didn't want to say she was Steve's wife's twin sister. "Why don't we have a night out like the old days. Do you think you could make Saturday mate?" "I could" "I will call Steve, where do you want to meet?" "What about the Wobbly Man, has Rick still got it?" "Yes he has mate, ok, 7.30pm there then on Saturday" "Right, what do you want for your supper?" "Fish chips and mushy peas in a carton please, what do I owe you?" "Nothing mate, that's on the house, great to see you and will see you Saturday" "Thanks Derek" John left the little green

SERVED COLD

painted fish and chip van and
headed home.

DC could smell the fish and
wouldn't leave John alone. He
broke a bit off the fish and put it
down to get some rest from her
attention but she was soon back
wanting more. John gave up and
gave the rest of the fish to the
cat and made four chip
sandwiches with mushy peas.
So tomorrow, he thought what
was the Survivors meeting going
to be about? He hoped he would
get some kind of lead from it.
Finishing his sandwich, he
showered and jumped into bed,
it wasn't long before DC joined
him licking her lips, she
obviously enjoyed Derek's fish
he thought.

SERVED COLD

Chapter 2

The following morning he drove
into work. There was a lot of
activity in the station when he
arrived. "What's going on
Magic?" "Just this minute took a
call from a man out walking who
spotted something in the bushes
at Dumpling Dale sir" "What?"
"A body apparently, DI Milton
has gone to the scene and Wally
and his team are on their way"
"Ok, thanks Magic" "Morning
Sir" "Yes, Morning Kate, don't
take your coat off we have a body
to go and look at" "Oh lovely sir"
Gammon took Kate and they
headed for Dumpling Dale. They
parked in the windswept car park
and in the distance they could see
Wally's tent. "Not quite got the
correct shoes for yomping in the

SERVED COLD

Peak District sir" "Well that will teach you Kate" and Gammon laughed as he strode off across Dumpling Dale. Wally saw Gammon coming and met him outside the tent instead of having to lecture him about scene contamination. "What have we got Wally?" "A male I would say, twenty- five or maybe thirty, tattooed again which I am guessing will be the same ink as the previous one. This man was badly beaten John, he has bruises everywhere and I mean everywhere, whoever did this, before they killed him, took him to within an inch of his life. That's your lot for now Mr Gammon so, yes, I will have a report for 9.00 am in the morning incident meeting" "Thanks Wally you are a star" Gammon then

SERVED COLD

wandered over to DI Milton and DS Bass who were talking to a man who Gammon assumed had found the body.

"Good morning are you the gentleman that contacted Bixton about the body?" "Yes" "Your name please sir" "Willis, Gerald Willis, I was out running when I saw a foot stick out of the bush over there so I went over to investigate and found that gentleman" "Did you touch the body sir?" "No, I told your colleagues I immediately called Bixton Station, I had the number in my phone because two weeks ago my wife reported a robbery at the supermarket where she works and she came in to do a statement and I went in with her. We met with a Detective Inspector Lee" "Oh, ok then Mr Willis, if we

SERVED COLD

need to see you again if you
would be kind enough to give
your address to DI Milton"
"Come on Kate, let's get back to
Bixton, nothing more we can do
here"
"Have you had anything to eat
today?" "No sir, why?" "Come
on then, I will take you to a
famous café" "Oh sounds great,
what's it called?" "It's called the
Wriggly Tin because of its tin
roof" Gammon took her the
scenic route which took in some
of the most fantastic views. They
arrived at the Wriggly Tin Café
and sat by the little window.
"Look over there sir, they are
abseiling off that viaduct" "Yes
it's quite a big thing up here"
The waitress came to the table,
"What would you like?" "Well I
would like the Wriggly Tin spud

SERVED COLD

please" "With everything sir?"
"Yes please" "Could I have the
bacon viaduct please?" "What
drinks would you like?" "The
strongest black coffee for me
please" "I'll have a lemon tea
please"

"So Kate, how are you?" "It's
been quite hard since we lost
Danny Kiernan, we hadn't been
together long but we really got on
well" "So do you have a new
love?" "Well I wouldn't say love
but I am seeing Carl, DI Milton"
"Oh that's good, he has been
through the ringer these last few
years, I'm pleased for you both"
The drinks and the food arrived.
"Blimey, what have we ordered?"
"Well my spud has cheese,
bacon, beans, spring onion and
mashed cauliflower, they scoop
the potato out of the jacket mix it

SERVED COLD

all together then put it back"
"Blimey, I have never seen a
potato that big sir" "So what does
your bacon viaduct have?" "Well
it's a crosspatch of bacon then a
layer of mashed potato then
another layer of bacon then fresh
tomatoes, onion, and their special
Wriggly Tin sauce then another
layer of bacon. Blimey sir, I
won't be fit for anything after this
lot" They both set about their
food. "Can I ask you a personal
question sir?" "Sure, fire away
Kate" "What made you come to
the Peak District? everyone
knows you were a very
successful detective in London"
"Well it's a long story, I was in a
marriage that wasn't working
well, my parents lived here and I
was asked to help on a serial
killer case so I just thought why

SERVED COLD

not" "So you ended up staying?"
"Well that is another long story
which I'm not going into" "Your
girlfriend is that pretty girl that
owns the Tow'd Man isn't it?"
"We are off and on Kate" "Oh
right, sorry for being nosey, I
don't know when to stop do I?"
"Don't worry about it, you are a
detective, that's why.
With the food finished they
headed back to Bixton. Gammon
liked to get to know his officers,
he felt it made for a more bonded
team. Once back at the station
Gammon headed for his office
and the daily drudge of his
paperwork which he hated, this
was the only part of the job he
really didn't like. Gammon
scribbled on his note pad "second
victim tattooed same as first
victim" Do we have a Jewish

SERVED COLD

hater were these people actually Jews or British and born here? He decided once they had the second victims name he would get DS Bass to look in to where they were born.

The following morning Gammon was in for 8.00 am, he wanted to get a head start on the paperwork before the 9.00am meeting as he knew he would be vising somebody once the name of the latest victim was known. He climbed the stairs and noticed Kate Bass's office that she shared with DI Smarty had the light was on so he put his head round the door. "Oh, good morning Kate, you are in early" "I usually get in about 7.45am sir" Gammon then realised it would always be before him.

SERVED COLD

"Oh, great Kate, I'll let you crack on then, don't forget the 9.00 am meeting" "I'll be there sir" Gammon grabbed a coffee and sat at his desk looking at the enormous amount of paperwork he had to wade through.

By 9.00am he had only managed to make a small dent in the paperwork mountain, he headed for the meeting. "Ok everyone, yesterday we had another victim so hopefully Wally has some news for us" "Ok, the victim was a white male aged somewhere between twenty-five and thirty with a tattoo on his upper left breast, B20081, same ink as the previous victim and the tattoo artist I would say is very much an amateur. He was taken to where he was found, he was not killed there. There was

SERVED COLD

very little food in his stomach so
my guess is he was being
starved to death, the cause of
death was a blow to the back of
the head with a blunt instrument,
quite possibly a lump hammer of
some sort.

This man was on the police
database for Activists, it's one
we don't talk about but know it
goes on. He was campaigning
for the return of Jewish gold and
artefacts known to still be in
Swiss banks, his name was Josef
Guran and his address was
Number eleven Reservoir Way
near Winksworth. We did find
DNA on him that wasn't his but,
like the previous victim, we are
having no joy finding a match"
"Thanks Wally, right, we have
two victims both with some
association with the Jewish

SERVED COLD

Community yet our first victim was dating a known Nazi sympathiser, work that one out if you can, so we have Victim one, Ruth Weisner, worked at Laskey's biscuits, DI Smarty I would like you to take DS Yap and see what you can dig up on Ruth at the biscuit factory, DS Bass, you concentrate on looking into Ruth's affairs, friends she had, you know the usual stuff.

We know victim two was a male, Josef Guran, we believe he is a youth worker again with ties to the Jewish Community, DI Milton, you get looking into Guran please.

Possible Suspect Marty Baynes, known Nazi Sympathiser but lived with Ruth Weisner, DI Lee

SERVED COLD

you look into our friend Mr
Baynes please.

I'm going to break the news to
Josef Guran's family, let's meet
up in the morning and share
what we have please, say
9.00am"

Gammon headed for
Winksworth, he knew the
cottages because an old friend of
his mum's lived at the end
cottage for many years and she
would take John and Adam to
see her, she was quite an old
lady when they were about ten
so John and Adam would tidy
the garden and chop sticks for
her.

Gammon pulled into the small
area set aside for residents to
park their cars at the end of the
row and he walked down to
number eleven. All the cottages

SERVED COLD

had been done up over the years
and were probably worth a lot of
money now with the fabulous
reservoir in view.

A woman in her early thirties
answered the door of number
eleven. Gammon showed his
warrant card. "May I come in?"
"Yes, what is this about?" She
showed Gammon into the small
living room with its tremendous
view of the reservoir. "I'm
afraid I have some bad news
Mrs Guran" "Oh my name is
Abigail Harrop, me and Josef
just live together since his
mother died" "Oh, ok, well
Abigail I'm afraid your husband
was found at Dumpling Dale, he
had been severely beaten then
murdered" "Abigail Harrop sat
in the leather winged chair. "Are
you sure Mr Gammon? he had

SERVED COLD

gone to Whitby for a week's
fishing, it was a surprise for an
old friend he has up there" "I'm
sorry but we have DNA from
Josef from a previous incident,
he never went to Whitby if that's
where he was heading.
So, the last time you saw Josef
was when exactly?" "It will be
five days ago today" "Did he
seem worried about anything?"
No, not really, Josef was a
considerate man, always
thinking about others, he worked
tirelessly for the Jewish
community, his grandparents
were very rich but the Nazi's
took it off them. Josef's father
told him about the gold and he
has traced it with others from
The Jewish community to a
Swiss bank but that was

SERVED COLD

eighteen months ago and he is feeling frustrated about that" "Does he meet up with the Jewish community?" "Yes he is a member of the Jewish Survivors Club, they meet in Ackbourne on the second Friday of every month" Abigail had stopped crying so Gammon felt ok with the questioning.
"What exactly does the club do?" "Well, let's say I wanted to buy a small shop, you can get a loan from the elders with no interest and you pay them back, that's one thing they do. We have families over from Russia because they suffered greatly and still do to some degree" "When you say we Abigail do you attend these meetings?" "Yes Mr Gammon, have done for a long time, I was a youth

SERVED COLD

worker in Cramford when I met Josef and he introduced me to the Jewish community, they are lovely people and do so much for the community all year round" "I'm sorry to have to ask you this but we do need the body of Josef formally identified tomorrow" "Ok Mr Gammon, I'm sure one of the elders will want to come with me so I will be ok" "Just one last thing, whoever is carrying out these murders is also tattooing the victim, does this number B20081 mean anything to you?" "It's an Auschwitz tattoo number Mr Gammon" "Ok, thank you Abigail, I may be in touch again as the case progress's, I am very sorry for your loss, here is my card if you think of anything that may help

SERVED COLD

catch the killer, even the smallest of detail, contact me day or night" "Thank you Mr Gammon"

It was now almost 3.00pm as John left the cottage so he phoned Saron. "Hi, you ok?" "What do you think?" "Have you called the doctors for the test?" "Not yet, I have been too busy" "Saron this is important for all of us" "I know, I will do it now and call you back" John was a bit annoyed that Saron hadn't arranged the doctor's appointment but that was just the way Saron seemed to roll currently.

He was almost at Bixton when Saron rang back. "Only slot they had is 4.30pm tomorrow John so I booked it" "Ok I will meet you at Hittington Surgery" Saron

SERVED COLD

hung up, John knew by her actions she was dreading the thought it might not be his and he was no different, if it was his then Saron would want them to be together.

John landed at Bixton and got straight into his paperwork. It was almost 7.45 when he finally had something resembling a desk instead of a paper mountain. He said goodnight to Di Trimble on the desk and left deciding on heading for The Spinning Jenny. On the way he called Steve and said about meeting with Derek Lolly in the Wobbly man. Steve was up for that and said India would pick john up and they could have taxis. "Sounds great mate will be good to all meet up"

SERVED COLD

John then phoned Derek and said it was all arranged and could he get his wife to drop him off and they would have taxis everywhere, Derek said there would not be a problem with that. "See you Saturday night about 7.30pm at the Wobbly Man Derek"

John walked in the Spinning Jenny and Lindsay was stood with Chocolate with Wez behind the bar. Good evening Mr Gammon they all said. "What are you drinking John?" "Usual Pedigree mate please" "Have you heard our Chocolate's good news?" "No, what's that Lindsay?" "She has bought that café in Swinster and she is turning it into a wine bar with her friend Amelia from Barnsley" "Oh wow, so you are

SERVED COLD

coming to live down here then Chocolate?" "That's the plan, we are turning the café into a bistro and wine bar, we won't be in competition with Lindsay it will be different clientele" "What are you going to call it?" "We have two names, I like "In the Dog House" and Amelia likes "Blooming Bonkers" "Think I like In The Dog House what about you Lindsay?" "I'm with you John on that." "Well good luck Chocolate, I'm sure whatever you name the business it will be successful" "Thank you John"

John wandered over to Jack and Shelley. "How are you two?" "Good John, the bed and breakfast is booming. Did I hear correct Claire is opening a Bistro and Wine bar in Swinster

SERVED COLD

village?" "Yes with a friend from Barnsley" "Oh that should be nice and not far for us to travel Jack" "I prefer a proper pub like this one, real ales hey John?" "I'm happy with both Jack to be honest" "I was talking to my lad, he went to the Blood Tub him and some mates" "Where is that?" "Tow'd Holes, well just outside" "Oh you mean the Gibbet, blimey is that still going? it's the only pub I know that won't sell lager, I think the landlord was Arthur Green" "Yeah well it's his son Bert now, he is his double John, pub is exactly how it was years ago" "I'm going out with Steve Saturday night and we are meeting in the Wobbly Man with an old school friend so we

SERVED COLD

will have to try the Gibbet,
forgot all about it"
"Why was it called the Gibbet?"
"I know that Mr Gammon" "Go
on then Shelley, enlighten me"
It's where people were hung in a
metal basket, quite often just left
to die with no food and water, it
was supposed to be a deterrent,
people would come from miles
away out of morbid curiosity.
They reckon in seventeen fifty-
one a famer called Shadrack
Yeoman turned his living room
into an ale house and that's how
the pub came about. I am
surprised it's still open because
there are no houses for about a
mile but again people go for the
curiosity of the place I guess
John" "Thanks Shelley, you
learn something new every day.
Why did your lad call it the

SERVED COLD

Blood Tub?" "Well apparently those they did kill bled to death and the old farmer collected the blood in a tub and they reckon his cows would drink it" "Oh blimey, perish the thought hey mate"

The following day at the incident room meeting some interesting information came forward. "Everybody listen up, let's start with DS Bass, what have you got on Ruth Weisner?" "She, as we know, worked at Laskeys' biscuit factor, prior to that she had been in the theatre but apparently she was named in a divorce case by some high-flying theatre director and she was black balled by theatre land so with no job she went on quite a slide and ended up in those dreadful apartments and met

SERVED COLD

Baynes. I think she may also have been shunned by the Jewish community for her infidelity and maybe being seen with Baynes was a way of putting to fingers up to them" "Interesting analogy Kate, well done.

Dave what have you and Ian found out at Laskey's?" "Not a great deal to be honest, she hadn't worked there long and we did get the impression the factory girls thought that she thought the job was below her" "Ok thanks Dave, Ian, "Ok Carl your turn" "Josef Guran was a very passionate man well liked in the Jewish community, from what I could get out of some of the elders his grandparents had been very rich before the war but had all their gold and family

SERVED COLD

heirlooms taken from them, his grandparents had also been in Auschwitz but survived, so there is a common thread here sir, both sets of grandparents were in Auschwitz and both survived because we know Weisner's grandparents were also there. My feeling is our killer has some association or his ancestors do with the concentration camps. I also found out that Gurans parents and grandparents committed suicide, his grandparents in nineteen fifty-four and his parents two years ago, why we don't know, there were no letters left"

"Ok DI Lee, what about our star suspect?" "Baynes had been done for the attempted manslaughter of a black kid, he spent time in jail. We know he is a member of HRP 33 a Nazi group of skinheads and he quite revels in it around the town apparently. The witness at his trial, one Robert Falcon recruited him as soon as he got out of prison. Falcon is known to the authorities and Special Branch and is a nasty piece of work but also clever, he lets his minions get their hands dirty, that way he stays out of the limelight. These thugs all drink in the Broken Donkey in Ackbourne where Falcon holds court"

"Ok I want Baynes brought in on any trumped-up charge you like, I want that mans' DNA. I'll leave that with you DI Lee and DI Smarty, just let me know when you have him please"

SERVED COLD

Gammon came out of the incident room. "Sir, I've got Jeremy Goldwing MP for the High Peak on the phone for you" "Ok, put him through to my office please Magic" "Good morning, DI Gammon speaking how can I help you?" "Mr Gammon, Jeremy Goldwing Member of Parliament for The High Peak, I wanted to touch base with you for a couple of reasons. I was speaking with a fellow MP, Mr Liam Charlton Member of Parliament for Derbyshire Dales, he has concerns that his Jewish community are being singled out for unnecessary attention by Bixton Police and I said I would have a word to find out what the problem is" "Well Mr Goldwing, the problem is I have

SERVED COLD

two unsolved murders on my
hands and if speaking with the
Jewish community or the damn
Nazi group he has in his town
upsets or ruffles a few feathers
then I'm afraid my stance is,
carry on regardless"
"Mr Gammon I am a little
shocked at your tone, with
regard to the cases I fully
understand the police have a job
to do but there is a way to go
about things without upsetting
long standing communities who
my colleague represents" "Is
there anything else Mr
Goldwing as I have a busy day"
"I will speak with the shadow
Home Secretary over dinner
tonight DI Gammon and I will
be in touch" and he slammed the
phone down. Tosser, thought
Gammon.

SERVED COLD

The following day John met Saron at Hittington surgery for their test. Doctor Gillespie explained that he needed a blood sample from Saron's arm and John could either give a hair sample mouth swab sample or blood, he chose blood, John knew that would be the most reliable.

"Ok, well that's done, if you call the surgery sometime after 4.00pm on Monday we should have the DNA results" "Thank you" and he showed Saron and John out. Of all the people he didn't want to see it was Carol Lestar. "Hello John, hi Saron, I'm just here with mum for her check-up, what you two been up to, not AI is it? I know a farmer who will do it for free" and she laughed making the old lady that

SERVED COLD

was almost asleep in the corner
suddenly take notice.

John and Saron hurried out of
the surgery and for the first time
Saron did laugh. "That was just
our luck hey John?" He could
tell she seemed a bit more
relaxed now the test was done
because at least she would
know. The thing John was
concerned about was if the baby
was his then he had a second
chance of being a family with
Saron, if it wasn't, what if
Paddy wanted Saron and she did
it for the good of the baby?"
"Do you want to go for a meal
Saron?" "No, I have to get back
John, its Donna's night off"
John decided he would go home
and try and clear his head, it was
while he was sat watching a
history program on BBC iPlayer

SERVED COLD

that he suddenly remembered the lady saying she had seen an range Fiat Panda racing from the first murder, he quickly called DS Bass and told her to look on Monday morning at all owners of orange Fiat Pandas registered in the Peak District.

With the weekend now here, John did some jobs around the house, not that there was much to do as Phyllis Swan did everything for him. India and Steve picked him up at 7.00pm and they drove down to Toad Holes. It was a beautiful night with a full moon, the moonlight highlighted the beautiful village of Toad Holes.

"There you go boys, have a nice evening" "Thanks India" "No problem John just don't get him into any trouble" and she

SERVED COLD

laughed. "It's the other way around India" Steve retorted. "Can't wait to see old Shilling" "Oh I forgot we used to call him Shilling because of his surname Lolly!!"

Sure enough Shilling was sat at the bar chewing the fat with Rick Hieb and already half way down his first pint of Stella. "Hey how are you Shilling?" "Bloody Pandashell Lineman packed a bit of Pork on me old lad" "It's the good living mate" "What are you two having?" "I'll have a Witches Brew". "What about you John?" Same please Derek" "I can't believe all these years later we are sat in the Wobbly having a beer and all of us back here after our travels" "So Derek where have you been these last

SERVED COLD

twenty odd years?" "About fifteen years back I was working in Crete on a pipeline, welding" "Oh yeah, you used to work for Greaves at Cramford didn't you?" "Yeah mate, went there straight from school" "Anyway, they got a government job in Crete so I was working out there and met Molly my wife, she was a rep for Thomas Cook, anyway long story short we made our home there, she carried on being a tour rep and I did odd jobs and worked behind a bar, then Molly had some health issues so we came back and I bought the chip van" "Do you know, I have seen that chip van in Swinster and often said to India we should try it, what a bloody coincidence Derek" "Life is full of surprises Steve"

SERVED COLD

Three pints in and the lads were full of stories from their teenage years. "Rick, will you get us a taxi to the Gibbet please?" "No problem mate but are you sure? he is a miserable old so and so" "Not a problem mate, we are on a pub crawl" "Ok" Within five minutes the taxi had arrived and they were on their way to the Gibbet. The car park was empty, not surprising seeing where the pub was situated, you needed a four by four, the poor taxi driver was moaning about his springs on his car. John gave him an extra fiver and asked if he would fetch them when he called, seeing that he was getting extra the little taxi driver soon forgot about the suspension springs on his car.

SERVED COLD

They walked in the Gibbet, it was a small pub with very low ceilings with oak beams everywhere. The bar was solid oak with carvings depicting the gruesome way they killed people and left them in the Gibbet as a deterrent. "Where are the beer pumps John?" "Think he gets it in a jug from the cellar" "What beer have you got landlord?" "The name's Bert if you want to drink here" "Oh sorry Bert" "I have Flossy Top and Drunken Dog" "Do you have lager Bert?" Now that was a mistake from Derek thought John.

"I don't sell girls beer, if you want that try one of the pubs in the village, now make your mind up" Not that Bert was busy just he was a grumpy guy. "Best have three Flossy Tops then

SERVED COLD

please Bert. How much are your
pork pies here on the bar?" "If
you have to ask you can't afford
one" That quietened Steve.
He came back up from the cellar
with a big aluminium jug full of
beer and promptly poured the
three pints. "We will take three
pork pies as well please" "That's
fifteen pound ninety pence"
Steve handed him a twenty -
pound note. "Have you not got
anything smaller?" Derek almost
choked on his beer. "Is there a
problem lad?" "Oh sorry, no, it
went down the wrong hole that's
all" Steve apologised at giving
him a twenty- pound note. Bert
came back with the pork pies
and the change then promptly
filled his glass with what was
left in the jug. "So what are you
lads doing here?" Because of

SERVED COLD

how Bert was Steve wanted to
say drinking but knowing Bert's
lack of personality he thought
best not too.

"Just old mates, been away and
now all back living round here"
"I know your face" Bert said
pointing to John. "Have you
been in prison Bert?" "Why is
he a convict?" "No, a police
officer" "That's it, you are that
one that is always in the news
from Bixton aren't you?"
"Guess so" "What you doing
about these two people that have
been murdered?" "Sorry Bert, I
don't talk shop in my free time"
Probably the first time in his life
that Bert had been knocked
back, he left them at the bar and
sat with his border collie by the
roaring log fire.

SERVED COLD

"Where next Steve?" "Let's have one more call for a taxi and get him to take us to the Wop and Take, I like that pub" John tried to phone for a taxi but had no signal Steve ordered three more beers. "Any chance we can use your landline Bert?" "Ok but it's twenty pence a minute" Steve laughed and handed him a fifty pence piece and said keep the change.

"Do you still farm Bert?" "I've got about seven hundred sheep at the minute" "My dad was a dairy farmer until he passed away" "What were his name lad?" "Phil Gammon" "Well bloody hell, I used to always have a sausage roll and a pint with Phil on market day, lovely man salt of the earth. Bet tha knows Sheba Filey dos tha?"

SERVED COLD

"Yeah, I know Sheba very well, good friend of mine" Lineman poked Derek Lolly in the side as much to say more than a good friend. "She is my distant cousin" Next Bert turned to the spirits on the shelf and poured three very large whiskies.

"Here, tha should have said, have these on house, they are Speyside malt, bloody lovely" Just then the taxi guy arrived so they had to drink up quick. They thanked Bert and he shouted "Pop in again lads" as they left the low beamed bar to Bert and his dog.

Derek was by now a little tipsy as they entered the Wop and Take, it was very busy, they had a Cher impersonator singing. They eventually got served but decided to have the one then

SERVED COLD

head for Ackbourne. The taxi driver had hung on so John said there would be a big tip if he picked them up from Ackbourne Market Place at 1.30am. "Come on Porky, let's try the Twisted Card Player" they walked in and bumped straight into Jack and Shelly with Bob and Cheryl. "What are you lads doing?" "Pub Crawl Jack, we tried the Gibbet, certainly an experience." "They say he isn't bothered if he serves you or not" "Jack, by the time old silver-tongued Gammon had done he was giving us free drinks and inviting us back" "He is a natural Steve" "Sure is Shelley" and they both laughed. "Come on Cheryl, let's have a drink with the lads" "Ok with me Bob" They went back in with

SERVED COLD

the lads and found a corner seat
near the window. Poor Derek
was about half way down his
pint when he just fell asleep.
"Blimey you two certainly did
him. Isn't he the guy that sells
fish and chips from a van?"
"Yes, we were mates years ago
then he moved to Crete"
"What's his name?" "Derek
Lolly" "Bloody hell, that's never
old Shilling is it? He must have
had a heavy paper round, he
hasn't fared to good" "It will be
all that sun in Crete, it ages you
Bob"
Four drinks later and the taxi
pulled up, luckily he had come
in a mini-bus so they managed
to get everyone home, even poor
old Derek who for the last hour
was drinking copious amounts
of strong black coffee.

SERVED COLD

Chapter 3

Sunday morning and John felt quite good for saying how much he had drunk the night before and then not got to bed until almost 3.00 am by the time the driver had dropped everyone off. John decided to do a five mile walk then call at the Spinning Jenny for one of Lindsay super Sunday lunches.

Leaving the farm he headed on towards Cuckoo Dale, it wasn't one of the most dramatic Dales but it was easy walking, by the time he had got there then walked back towards Swinster and the Spinning Jenny it was almost 1.20pm. "Hey John, how did your session go last night?" "Good mate, tried a few pubs and I'm just blowing the cobwebs off, any chance of a

SERVED COLD

Sunday lunch?" "Do you want it in the restaurant or the bar mate.?" "I'll have it in the restaurant for a change" "Ok, it's ordered now, pint of Pedigree?" He was ready to order another one when Wez said to go through and he would bring his beer through.

John sat down and Chocolate came through in her petite waitress uniform, she put John's dinner in front of him then sat down opposite him. "So Mr Gammon, what do you reckon to the Bistro/Wine bar idea.?" "Yes, it should work I think Chocolate, when do you hope to have it up and running?" "Well, we have ordered tables, cutlery a new large cooker all the things we will need and they should be delivered by mid-week. My

SERVED COLD

friend moves down here next week, she has sold her house in Barnsley"

"Which name did you go for?"

"We decided to call it the Dog House, it's after my dad Syd who is always saying he is in the Dog house like our Nellie" "I like that" "Yeah, Phil who comes in here knows some sign writer and he is getting them really reasonable for us" "Phil Sterndale?" "Yeah that's him, comes in with a lady called Linda" "Oh great, well sounds like you have it sorted" "You'd better bring your Saron down when we open" "Ok that's a deal" "I'd best crack on John or I will be getting the sack" and she laughed leaving John to the biggest plate of food, three slices of lamb, three slices of beef then

SERVED COLD

the usually mash and roast
potatoes, green beans,
cauliflower, carrots, brussel
sprouts and numerous sauces all
in small jugs.

John finished his meal and could
hardly move, he went back in
the bar and ordered a brandy, it
was now 4.00pm and Chocolate
came through. "Was your meal
ok John?" "More than ok, really
enjoyed it, not sure I can walk
home though, think I best get a
taxi" "I'll drop you off if you
want, nothing else on this
afternoon" "Are you sure
Chocolate?" "Yes, not a
problem, give me a shout when
you want to go"

John had two more brandies
then asked Chocolate for the lift
back. They drove down to his
cottage and the farm. "Wow

SERVED COLD

John, this is beautiful, what stunning scenery, how long have you lived here?" "Been back a few years but was brought up on this farm then when my parents died I converted the outbuildings and made holiday cottages and then moved into this one. Would you like a drink before you go back?" "Another time John, said I would help Lindsay with cleaning up in the kitchen" "Ok, well thanks Chocolate, I owe you one.

She drove away and John was met by DC who was beginning to resemble a full-grown cat now. He showered and decided to have an early night but it wasn't going to be on his own with DC about. The following morning he headed for Bixton and hopefully a lead on the killer and he hoped for a

SERVED COLD

lead on the orange Fiat Panda from DS Bass. "Morning Magic, quiet night?" "Yes sir, nothing to report" He climbed the stairs and Kate Bass was waiting with a coffee for him. "Got some information on the orange Panda sir" "Blimey that was quick Kate" "I came in Saturday and Sunday, I knew it was important" "Appreciate that Kate"

John took of his coat and sat at his desk. "Sir, there are seven orange Fiat Pandas but only two that are 61 Plates, both are UAC 61 but one finishes in BLM and one is KLP." "Ok, where are they from?" "One is registered to a Mary Tidings of Winksworth the other is for a Michael Mitchell of Derby" "Ok tell DS Yap and DI Lee to check the Wirksworth one and tell DI Smarty and DI Milton

SERVED COLD

to check the Derby one" "Ok sir"
"I want some urgency on this
Kate, I need answers before close
of play today"

Gammon took a call from the
chief of police asking for an
update on the murders and did
John feel they were getting close.
He knew if he said they were still
a million miles away that would
send the chief constable into a
spin and that's when they get all
this help which usually turns out
to be no help at all. "We are
getting closer sir, we are chasing
up a car seen at the first murder,
we have narrowed it down to two
possible vehicles and hopefully I
will know more by tonight" "Ok
John well keep me up to speed, I
am having to leave early today,
we have a black tie charity dinner
in the city speak soon" and the

SERVED COLD

phone went dead. Like he is interested Gammon thought, there was no way he would be calling him.

It was 4.40pm when they got back from the car checking. DI Lee confirmed that Mary Tidings vehicle had been in her garage for almost two weeks, she was the only person with a set of keys and her daughter who lived with her confirmed she had been off work for the last four weeks with a bad back that was why she was at the house, she had come to look after her and she didn't drive. "I checked her name address etc and she does not have a licence, think we can write that one off" "What about you Dave?" "It gets worse, the Fiat Panda in Derby was in a head on collision in Burton three weeks ago and was written off by the insurance company and I'm afraid it wasn't even driveable" "Has it had gone up in flames? Crap, I was hoping for something out of one of these lads, Ok, back to the drawing board I guess, thanks"

Gammon finished off his paperwork, it was now 5.40pm, he had got so engrossed in the job he had forgotten to call Saron about the DNA test. He quickly got to his car away from the prying eyes and immediately rang Saron. Her phone rang twice then she answered. "John why haven't you called? The bloody job got in the way again of something this important" "Look I'm sorry just calm down, shall I come up?" "Well I think that would be a good idea don't you?" "Ok I'm

SERVED COLD

on my way" John was annoyed
with himself, he could see her
point. He drove quickly to get to
the Tow'd Man, when he walked
in the bar Kathy Vickers was
working the bar. "Hi Kathy, you
seen Saron?" "It's her night off
John, I'm guessing she is in her
apartment" "Is it ok to go up?" "I
guess so" John went out the back
way up to Saron's apartment and
knocked on the door.
"Come in" she shouted. John
went into Saron's apartment, it
was always immaculate, never
anything out of place. "Hey, you
ok?" He could see she had been
crying. "So, are you going to tell
me?" "It's yours John, the baby is
yours" John sighed with relief
then he hugged Saron. "Why the
tears?" "Bloody relief you nutter"
"I'm lost for words sweetheart,

SERVED COLD

I guess we have to decide what to do then" "Will if you mean termination there is no way I'm doing that" "No, no of course not, I don't mean a termination, are you kidding? I am over the moon" "Oh good, so what do you mean?" "Well, what part would you like me to play in its life and how does this affect us?" "Let's go out and discuss this, I can drink orange juice" "Ok I'll take you to The Black Bess in Biffin by Hittington, should be quiet there" "Ok let me put some make up on and change my clothes" John sat thinking what Saron had in mind hoping she was going to say they should live together then hopefully get married before she has the baby. His heart was racing thinking he was going to

SERVED COLD

be a dad; his mum would have been so pleased for him. "Ok John, you ready" "Wow, being pregnant suits you" "Why is it showing?" "No just joking, you always look stunning" They drove to the Black Bess, it was a rainy evening so the car park was empty, perfect John thought.

They walked into the little bar and it was empty but of course there is always somebody about when you need to talk. Steve Condray and Fiona Scott were stood at the bar. "Hey Mr Gammon, how are you?" "Yes good thanks Steve" "You have met Fiona haven't you?" "No sorry don't think we have met" "Oh sorry, Fiona this is the famous John Gammon and Saron from the Tow'd Man.

SERVED COLD

What are you two drinking?"
"No, you are ok thanks Steve,
only having a quick one" "So
come on, what are you having?"
"Ok I'll have a pint of Farmer
Giles please" "Saron what
would you like?" "Oh, just an
orange juice please" "Blimey,
you aren't watching your figure
are you? If there is one person
who doesn't need to do that it's
you" Steve said in a flirty way
which made Fiona gave him a
stern stare.

John and Saron could not shake
Steve and Fiona off so no
conversation on the baby.
Eventually they managed to
leave saying Saron had to get
back to lock up. Steve was still
banging on about Saron's figure
as they left much to the

SERVED COLD

annoyance of Fiona and the embarrassment of Saron.

"If only he knew John" she said as they got on the car. "Do you want to stay at mine tonight and we can talk?" "Yes that would be nice" Back at the Tow'd Man they let Kathy Vickers leave, she said it had been quiet. John locked up while Saron made two coffees and said she would take them up.

They lay in bed both feeling awkward. "Look John, I want you to have as much time with our baby as you wish, there are no strings, I don't need support from you" "I know all that Saron, I was hoping this might get us together"

"Yes, I thought about that too but you are John Gammon!!" "What does that mean?" "John you are a

SERVED COLD

lovely guy in every sense but you can't resist a pretty face, I don't want to cover old ground but even on the eve of our wedding night you cheated on me"

"Saron that was before, I know I can change, I wanted this to be our chance, we can be a family, we can get a house and help if needed if you want to keep the pub on" "There you go John organising my life for me, why do you do that?" "I don't know, I could probably blame work, I am that used to organising I take it into my private life" "You see John we have two problems, you and other women and your job"

"Saron you have worked in the job so you know all about that and the women thing, you make me sound like a flippin gigolo" Saron laughed at that.

SERVED COLD

"Look let's stay as we are until the baby is born then if everything is still going well maybe then we can look at getting together as a family. I still want you to come to all the classes with me though" John cuddled her and lay listening to the rain beating down. He knew if he kept his nose clean he would have a great chance of settling with Saron.

The following morning she had made John a bacon sandwich and a strong black coffee just as he liked it. "I could get used to this sweetheart" "Well maybe you will" she said.

John left for work and Saron said she would be in touch, he decided to give Kev a ring and see if he would meet him for a pint that night. He knew if he

SERVED COLD

told Kev it would go no further and he was bursting to tell someone about the baby. Kev said make it about 5.45pm. Gammon arrived at work had a quick conversation with Magic on the front desk then sat in his office, he often doodled on a pad, it helped him think. He wrote "Jewish connection, WHY?" Gammon decided to call Abigail and see if he could go with her to the Jewish Survivors Club. She said it was ok and to meet her Friday at 8.00pm in Ackbourne, the meeting was held in room thirteen of the Town Hall so Gammon said he would meet her at the entry on Friday at 7.45pm.

He was hoping he might get some kind of help with the case,

SERVED COLD

he knew it was a long shot but at the moment he had nothing and anything would help.

All week nothing was coming to light then lunch time on the Thursday PC Magic rang his office, "Sir I have a man on the phone say's he needs to speak to you"
"Is that John Gammon?" "Yes, it is, how can I help you?" The man had a southern accent. "I need to tell you Mr Gammon that I am the killer of these people and it will carry on, I am not a murderer this is retribution which I will reveal on the last killing" "Look why don't you turn yourself in, maybe I can help you or do you want to meet?" The phone went dead, what the hell was that all about?

SERVED COLD

Chapter 4

When Friday night arrived John was desperate for some help with the case, he met Abigail Harrop outside Ackbourne Town Hall. John struggled to find somewhere to park so it was nearer 8.00pm when he arrived. "I had almost given up Mr Gammon, I thought you had changed your mind" "No, I am very sorry Abigail, I had trouble parking" "Not a problem Mr Gammon, lets go in" The Town Hall was very old and must have been very grand in its day, they climbed the sweeping staircase and walked down the marbled floor corridor to room thirteen, there was a piece of paper taped to the door which simply said Jewish Meeting.

SERVED COLD

Abigail led the way and introduced John to Morris Offing one of the Elders. "I believe you are a policeman Mr Gammon?" "Yes that's correct" "If we in our small group can help you please ask as many questions as you wish, as you know we represent our grand-parents and even our great grand- parents who survived the Holocaust"

"Yes Abigail has told me some bits" "Well first, join us in tea and apple cake or honey cake if you prefer" "Apple cake would be nice thank you" John figured there was about forty- five people present of all ages. Morris handed John the cake and he took a mouthful. "This is really nice, thank you" "Apple

SERVED COLD

cake is to wish you a sweet year
Mr Gammon"

"I'm sorry if I am somewhat
ignorant but what exactly does
your group do?" "Well there are
twelve elders, almost everybody
you see here today had a family
survivor from the Holocaust" It
was then that John noticed
pictures on the wall and a flag of
Israel draped over the table on
the stage. "We pray Mr
Gammon, we help each other
and we keep our ancestors' story
alive because it must never
happen again, you understand?
There are twelve Elders here
including me and, though I say it
myself, we do a good job for our
people. We arrange trips home
and we do work all year so that
survivors' families can go home
for two weeks at least every five

SERVED COLD

years. Anyway Mr Gammon,
after our meeting if you wish to
talk to some of the Elders you
are very welcome"

John sat at the back of the room
while people stood up
recounting what their parents
had told their families. They
sang then the twelve elders
asked if anybody needed help, a
couple were shown into a back
room. Joh was offered more tea
and eventually at 9.15pm the
meeting was closed, five of the
Elders stayed behind and invited
John into the back room. All
five men must have been in their
mid-eighties he thought. They
introduced themselves and the
sprightlier of them, a James
Sinclair, asked John what the
police were doing about the
murders from their group. "It is

SERVED COLD

like a bad penny, why are we being persecuted again and everyone is standing by and watching. Do you people never learn?" "Mr Sinclair we are throwing every resource we have at the case but as always we need help from the public. One of the reasons I am here tonight is to understand your group and try and find out why these people were targeted"

"Let me tell you why we are targeted Mr Policeman, because people like you stood by and let these atrocities happen"

"Calm down James, Mr Gammon is only trying to help" "You will never understand Asher Begin, you think the world has moved on" "We have to believe it has James" "Then you are a bloody fool, goodnight." and James

SERVED COLD

Sinclair walked out. "I am sorry Mr Begin, I didn't want to offend anyone" "James lost two brothers, his mother and father, only he and his sister survived the Holocaust Mr Gammon" "Look I think I may have caused enough upset Mr Begin, thank you for your hospitality" John shook his hand and left, Abigail must have already gone John thought as he walked down the marbled floor corridor to the sweeping staircase. Abigail was actually waiting at the bottom of the stairs. "I wanted to tell you that James Sinclair, one of the Elders isn't very friendly but when you went in the back room it was too late Mr Gammon"

"Yeah I can see he would be an acquired taste Abigail. Thank you for letting me come along, it

SERVED COLD

has been quite an eye opener"
John walked Abigail to her car
then set off looking for his, it
was almost 10.00pm now so he
just had time for a quick drink in
the Spinning Jenny.
John was quite shocked, there
was nobody in just Wez reading
an Aston Villa program. "At
last, a customer!" "Been that bad
Wez?" "Only the last hour mate,
from 4.00pm to 9.00pm we were
rammed then it just died I was
thinking of locking up but now
you are here I'd best have a
drink with you, my shout,
Pedigree John?" "Please mate"
"Why are you so late?" "Been
working" "I know I shouldn't
ask but any clues on these
murders?" "Hitting a brick wall
at the minute mate, it's
sometimes like that though to be

SERVED COLD

honest" "Wouldn't have you job
for all the tea in China John"
and Wez laughed as he went
back to his Villa program.
John just had two pints then left
so Wez could lock up, it wasn't
fair keeping the pub open just
for him.
Monday morning John headed
for work, he had just climbed
out of Dumpling Dale when his
phone got a signal, he had three
missed calls from DI Smarty.
John called him back. "What's
up Dave? only just got a signal"
"We have another body John,
another man. Wally is here with
me and DI Milton" "Where are
you mate?" "The Barrel at
Ropesmoor" "This early Dave?"
"Two dray men delivering beer
found a body pushed down the
cellar John" "Ok I'm on my

SERVED COLD

way" Ropesmoor was only just
in Gammon's area, much further
and it would have been
Staffordshire police's concern.
Gammon arrived, he could see
DI's Smarty and Milton talking
to two burly guys next to a lorry
with beer barrels on it. Wally's
white tent was blowing in the
wind. Gammon showed his
warrant card to the dray men.
"Who found the body?" "I did"
"And you are?" "Jimmy Gilbert"
"Ok Mr Gilbert, was the person
alive when you found him?"
"No he was definitely dead, I
was in the St John's Ambulance
for fifteen years so knew how to
check him"
"Ok Mr Gilbert, DI Smarty and
Milton will take all the details"
Gammon strode purposely over
to Wally's forensic tent, he was

SERVED COLD

just about to put his head into the tent when Wally stopped him. "What have we got?" "Male, late seventies I would say" "Had he been tattooed?" "Yes" "So is he another victim?" "Certainly looks like it John but I will be able to tell you in the morning" "Ok, I'm getting desperate mate, really need you to find something" "I'm convinced you think I am Harry Potter!!" "Well you sure seem to be able to pull tricks out of the hat my good friend" and John left Wally shaking his head.

He wandered back to Smarty and Milton. "Ok lads make sure we have full statements off the brewery lads and any other staff that were on duty last night, if possible, see if the landlord

SERVED COLD

knew any of the people that
were in last night and get some
names and if possible address's,
I'm going back to the station,
I'll see you later"
Gammon arrived back just has
he pulled into the car-park a blue
Fiesta pulled up alongside him,
he thought he recognised the car,
it was Abigail. "Oh hello Mr
Gammon" "Hi Abigail, you
ok?" "I have just been to see
Mrs Sinclair, she rang me
Saturday morning to ask if
James was at the meeting, I said
he had been and she said he
didn't come home and she was
worried about him. I told her to
report it to the police and if she
had heard nothing I would come
down on Monday to the station"
"James Sinclair, he was the guy
that left in a bit of huff wasn't he

SERVED COLD

Abigail?" "Yes, that's James. He is a very opinionated man Mr Gammon I really don't know how Myra puts up with him but they are both almost eighty and Myra isn't in good health, she says his time in the concentration camp formed the man he is Mr Gammon"

"Ok Abigail, follow me and we will see what my desk officer has to say" "Good morning PC Magic, this is Miss Harrop and she called in on Saturday about a missing person" "Let me have a look, I didn't do the desk on Saturday I had a day off, PC Hennessey stood in for me" Magic got the book out. Hennessy had logged the call at 10.40 am but had made the comment at the side "will inform PC Magic"." Why would

SERVED COLD

he put that Magic?" "Well I was only going to have the morning off then my wife persuaded me to have the day off, I did ring in but Hennessy had gone on his break and PC Fletcher took the call, I'm guessing the message didn't get passed on sir" Gammon was furious but had to be professional in front of Abigail. "Look Abigail I will personally look into this, I am very sorry for the mis-understanding" "He is an old man Mr Gammon, what if he has had an accident going home?" "Did he drive?" "No, he would have caught the 9.40pm bus back to Youtgreave, they live on a small farm, well, I suppose you would say small holding, just playing at being a farmer Mr Gammon"

SERVED COLD

Gammon could tell by the tone of Abigail's voice she wasn't a big fan of James Sinclair and was more concerned for his wife Myra.

"I'm very sorry for the delay in looking for Mr Sinclair Abigail, leave it with me, I will put all of my resources on it" Gammon knew as he was speaking that the body just found was most possibly Sinclair's and if not, it was a hell of a coincidence. Abigail left and Gammon told DS Yap to watch the desk he wanted Magic, Gillespie and Fletcher in his office.

All three came in looking sheepish, Gammon was fuming.

"How bloody irresponsible can you three be? An old guy goes missing Friday night, the station gets a call from his wife

SERVED COLD

Saturday to report it and the first thing we hear about it is when a friend of the family speaks with me in the car-park. Can you imagine my embarrassment when we realised what you clowns had done?" "Sir I feel that is a bit harsh, I took a day's holiday, I am entitled to holidays" "I'm telling you now all three of you, if you ever let something like this happen again I will drum you out of the force, now get out of my sight." "Sir do you want a search party arranging?" "Just get his name out, there is a fair chance the body found at Ropesmoor is James Sinclair so we are wasting resources now Magic"

The three constables left Gammon's office feeling battered and bruised, it was rare

SERVED COLD

for Gammon to lose his temper with his fellow officers but this could have been a major concern if indeed the body is James Sinclair and the media get hold of it.

Gammon carried on clearing his desk up until 5.30pm then he left and headed to the Tow'd Man. To John's surprise Saron was sat at the bar with Paddy laughing and joking, John really felt like he was playing gooseberry, he sat listening to them laughing, two- or three-times Paddy asked Saron if she would have a wine or something stronger than the flavoured water she was drinking. John stuck it until 7.30pm then made his excuses and left. Driving home, he felt annoyed that Saron had basically disrespected his feelings.

SERVED COLD

The following day they collected in the incident room. "Ok Wally, what have we got?" "We have a male, I would say very late seventies, he has been tattooed on the left- hand side of his chest with the number B20144, like the others the ink was made to look old but it has very recently been done. We have dental records that show the man is a Mr James Sinclair of Applegate Farm Youtgreave" "How was he killed Wally?" "A blunt instrument to the back of the head, we did find residue of duct-tape on his lips and wrist so this man was bound and gagged and taken, once he was dead, to Ropesmoor"

"Thank- you Wally" "Yes DS Smarty?" "The landlord gave us a list of customers that night, he

SERVED COLD

said they were all locals except for a couple he didn't know and a man playing darts with Charlie Thrusher a local" "Did you get Mr Trusher's address?" "Yes sir, Little Nook Farm, Ropesmoor" "Ok, DI Milton, DS Bass, DS Yap and DI Lee, split the list of locals up and go and question them, if you feel any of them may need further questioning then bring them in. Dave you come with, me let's go and talk to Charlie Thrusher but first we need to break the new of Mr Sinclair's death to his wife"

On the way Gammon rang Abigail Harrop, he thought she might like to be with Mrs Sinclair when he broke the bad news, Abigail said she would meet him at the farm.

SERVED COLD

Gammon knocked on the old white door which looked like it had been painted fifty years before, in fact the whole of the exterior of the house was in poor shape. The front garden had two goats wandering about eating anything in their way.

Abigail answered the door and gestured she hadn't said anything to Myra Sinclair. "This is Mr Gammon Myra from Bixton police, he wants to speak with you" "Oh pleased, to meet you Mr Bannon" "No, its Gammon Myra, you know like bacon, her hearing isn't great Mr Gammon" Gammon noticed on the fireplace a picture of a man in clothes at what looked like a concentration camp.

"Mrs Sinclair I am afraid we have some bad news for you"

SERVED COLD

Myra looked at Gammon
strangely so Abigail reiterated it.
"I'm afraid we have found Mr
Sinclair dead at Ropesmoor"
Again poor Myra didn't
understand. "She isn't taking it
in Mr Gammon" "Has she any
children?" "No, Mr Sinclair
didn't want any because of his
father" "Is that his father there?"
"Yes, he was in Auschwitz"
Abigail passed the picture of
James Sinclair to John, he could
see the resemblance and could
also just see some letters, he
could make out a two then a
zero. "Do you think I could
borrow the photograph?" "Can
Mr Gammon borrow the
photograph Myra?" She nodded.
"Thanks Abigail, it may help. Is
she going to be ok?" "Yes, I'm
here" "I feel really bad asking

SERVED COLD

this but somebody has to formally identify the body" "I will call Asher Begin and ask him to pop down tomorrow, I think I'd best stay with Myra for now Mr Gammon" "Ok then, we'd best get on" Gammon looked back at poor Myra, she hadn't cried or anything and he wondered if she actually understood. Abigail showed Gammon and Smarty to the door.

"Mr Gammon I don't want to speak ill of the dead but James Sinclair wasn't a nice man, it was rumoured that he used to beat Myra in the early days and whenever I was here he treated her like a dog" "Sounds like a lovely man hey Dave?" Smarty just nodded and they left Abigail at the door as they set off for

SERVED COLD

Ropesmoor and Charlie Trusher's place. "What are you thinking on the photograph John?" "I want see if our IT department can blow it up and enhance that number, I have a hunch Dave." "Are you going to let me in on it?" "Not yet mate but I will"

They parked at the side of the house and a guy, mid-thirties in wellingtons covered in cow muck came walking down. "You can't park that there this is private property" "Mr Trusher?" and they both produced their warrant cards. "Yes" "Charlie Trusher?" "Yes, what do you want? I have a hundred fifty cow's waiting to be milked" "Just a few questions sir, were you in the Barrel at Ropesmoor on Sunday night?" "Always am

SERVED COLD

why?" "Well we need to check a few things, what time did you leave?" "It was 10.10pm as usual, I like to get back for Match of the Day two" "Can anybody vouch for you?" "Well my wife will confirm I was home at 10.20pm oh and the guy I was playing darts with, he said his name was Marty, never seen him before, nice lad, good dart player" "Did this man have any tattoos?" "He had a swastika in the middle of his forehead, I asked him about it and he said it was something he did when he was fifteen, we all do daft things when we are young don't we?" "Ok Mr Trusher, thanks for your time" They climbed in the car. "I think the guy he played darts with was Marty Baynes, if so we have our prime suspect Dave"

SERVED COLD

"Our only bloody suspect John" and Smarty laughed.

Back at the station Gammon took the picture out of the frame and took it to the IT guy Richard Thomson, "Hi Richard, can you enhance this picture and blow it up?"

"Are there any specific area's you want me to concentrate on?"

"Yes, there on the man's arm, those numbers" "Ok leave it with me sir, give me an hour or so and I should be able to do something"

Gammon went back to his office and scribbled on his pad. "Why kill children and grand- children of Holocaust victims NO SENSE"

It was almost 3.50pm when Thomson came through with a blown -up picture of the man's

SERVED COLD

left arm, to Gammon's amazement the letter and number were the same tattooed on the victim as his father's B20114. "Thanks Richard that is a great help" Gammon decided to do some research, he found that the letter and number were only used in Auschwitz. Now he really had something, he needed to trace the other two victim's numbers just to clarify his suspicions that these were parents or looking, at the age of the victims, maybe Grandparents, but why?"

He decided to call at the Spinning Jenny and give Kev a call, he was quite into World War two and had read a lot about the Nazi's so he might be able to point him in the right direction. Kev said he would

SERVED COLD

meet him at 6.00pm at The Spinning Jenny as he was out shopping with Doreen and she would want a hand putting it away.

Gammon carried on with his paperwork, he would share what he had found with the team at the meeting the next day. Gammon left work at 5.40pm and headed to meet Kev. The Spinning Jenny was quite full but they found a spot in the window and John told Kev what he had found. Kev explained that the "A" prefix was for women and the "B" prefix was for men. He also told John that there was a Holocaust museum near Nottingham and they may have the number of his victims listed if indeed his theory was correct.

SERVED COLD

"Kev you are a star mate, I knew you would know" "I have my uses John" "Yeah, like putting shopping away for Doreen" and John laughed. "Cheeky monkey, what you drinking?" "I fancy a large red wine mate please" Kev ordered one for himself as well. "So come on then lad, what's troubling you?" John just blurted it out "Saron is expecting our child" Kev almost choked on his drink. Once he composed himself he congratulated John. "So are you and Saron going to make a go of it mate?" "Not sure Kev, I would but Saron is taking some convincing" "She will come around lad don't you worry" Kev said Doreen was picking him up at 10.00pm and that suited John as he didn't want to

SERVED COLD

be too late. They had a couple
more drinks and Doreen arrived
so John shouted goodnight to
Wez and left for the evening.
The following morning
Gammon told DI Smarty about
the Holocaust museum and
asked if he wanted to go with
him, he did so they headed off to
it. On the way Gammon told
Smarty that he thought that the
murdered victims were being
tattooed with the same number
as their relations but he didn't
know why. They arrived in the
small town of Menton and the
building that housed the
Holocaust Museum.
They paid the four pounds to get
in and an old lady in her late
seventies said the Holocaust
Museum was set up by a relative
of somebody that died in

SERVED COLD

Auschwitz, she wasn't a Jew herself but was so touched when she visited Auschwitz she said she had to do something to remember the people that suffered so dreadfully in the camps, her name was Rosie Lampley, she had since passed away and the lady showing Gammon and Smarty around was her sister in law Mary Lampley.

Gammon explained what he was looking for and Mary explained that they had hundreds of pictures and quite a few names of people that had been tattooed. Mary explained that it would take a few days to go through everything and she would have to ask a small charge for the research for the Museum as it was a charity. Gammon agreed

SERVED COLD

and gave her the numbers on the victims with their names.
"Ruth Weisner A 11407" "Josef Guran B 20081" and "James Sinclair B 20114" He also showed her the picture of Sinclair's father with the same number tattoo. Mary said she would get back to Gammon within a couple of days.
They left Mary with the information and headed back to Bixton. "Somebody has a grudge against the family members of some of the Holocaust victims of that I am sure Dave, once I saw the tattoo on Sinclair's father in the picture it started to fall into place"
Back at Bixton Gammon carried on the drudge of his paperwork, two days passed when he got a call from Mary at the Holocaust

SERVED COLD

museum. "I have some interesting findings Mr Gammon" "Brilliant Mary, please carry on"

"Right, well the first number you gave me of Ruth Weisner, the number she had tattooed on her chest A11407 was on our records as belonging to Madgar Genk who survived the Holocaust, the last record we have was that she was in France in 1946.

Josef Guran, the number tattooed B20081was originally on Herschel Marks, he also survived but there is no record of him once he was liberated.

James Sinclair, the number tattooed B20014 was originally on Ezra Sully, he also survived although once liberated was not heard of again.

SERVED COLD

You see Mr Gammon these
people had been to hell and
back, some had their tattoos
obliterated, some even
committed suicide, they couldn't
often live with the guilt that
maybe their family had been
murdered in the camps and they
had survived, also a lot changed
their names to try and fit back
into society"
"Thank you Mary I appreciate
your time and effort" "If you
need anything else Mr Gammon
just give me a call or pop down
and see us here" Mary hung up.
John now felt no further
forward, he was hoping for the
same name to pop up but this
was going to be a mammoth task
he thought.
John decided that the next day he
would call Abigail Harrop and

ask her if she would go with him to see Myra Sinclair again. He wanted to ask Myra about the photograph and could Ezra Sully be James Sinclair's father, had possibly either James or Ezra changed their surnames perhaps?

That night Gammon called Abigail hoping she would agree to a visit. "Of course Mr Gammon, can I ask why?" "I need to return the picture but I also want to ask Myra Sinclair some questions." "Ok, I can see you at Myra's say lunchtime perhaps?" "Thanks, see you there"

The following day he headed for Youtgreave and Applegate Farm to meet with Abigail and Myra. He knocked on the old farmhouse door to find Abigail crying. "Whatever is a matter

SERVED COLD

Abigail?" "Oh Mr Gammon, Myra has taken her life, I got here and found a bottle of whisky and these tablets all but gone, I called an ambulance but she was dead when they got here so I waited for you" "Oh I am sorry Abigail, why ever would she do that?" "I guess because she had lost James, love is a funny thing" "Ok, well I'd best get a team over just in case this isn't a suicide, was there a note left?" "Didn't see one Mr Gammon" By now Abigail had composed herself, "She was such a nice lady Mr Gammon" "How bad was her dementia?" "She had good days and bad I would say" "So you would assume this was possibly a good day, as crazy as that sounds" "I suppose so, that's the only way

SERVED COLD

she would have known what to
do Mr Gammon"
"Ok Abigail well you get off,
I'll take it from here" "What did
you want to know of Myra?
Maybe I can help" "Well the
man in the picture" "James'
father?" "Yes" "What about
him?" "Well it appears James
Sinclair was tattooed with the
same number as a man called
Ezra Sully" "Oh how dreadful"
"Did James or Myra ever say if
their name had been changed?"
"No Mr Gammon, not to my
knowledge, maybe it's just a
coincidence" "To be honest
Abigail we are clutching at
straws and it was a long shot.
Did Myra and James have any
family?" "Just a distant cousin
of James and I think he lived in
South America somewhere" "Oh

SERVED COLD

ok" "I will pay for their funeral
and sort the service out, it's the
least I can do for Myra, she must
have loved him for all of his
faults hey Mr Gammon?"
"Nothing so strange as love
Abigail"
John left Wally and the gang
checking over Myra it was
sitting uncomfortable with him
the death of this lady and
Abigail saying that Myra's
husband had a distant cousin in
South America started alarm bell
ringing.
He headed back to Bixton.
"Where's DS Bass?" "She is in
her office sir" "Ok Magic thank
you, get her to come to my
office please" Gammon climbed
the stairs to his office. DS Bass
was already stood waiting.
"Blimey Kate that was quick"

SERVED COLD

Bass laughed, "How can I help sir?" "Come into the office, I want you to look for somebody in South America for me" "Oh right, are you joking?" "No, seriously. The escape routes after World War two were called Ratlines, I want you to look for a surname "Sully", if you find any then we will go to the next stage" "Ok Sir, I will do my best"

"Thanks Kate" Bass left Gammon's office and headed down the corridor with no clue where to start looking for the name Sully.

Gammon's hunch that Sully was actually James Sinclair's father was a long shot but it was worth three or four days of DS Bass's time he thought.

SERVED COLD

That night John had classes with Saron, it was their first night as parents of the baby that Saron was carrying. He arranged to pick Saron up at 7.00pm at the Tow'd Man, Saron wasn't particularly showing John thought as she got in his car looking stunning as usual in a white pair of Jeggings a bright orange off the shoulder mohair jumper and a pair of orange flat shoes.

"Looking nice Saron, how have you been?" "Not too bad, a bit sick first thing in a morning and I get tired easily but Donna has been fantastic, she is fussing after me like a mother hen, the new girl, Kathy Vickers is really working out well, a real diamond behind the bar John.

SERVED COLD

What about you, how is work?"
"Not great, I thought I was on a good trail of our killer but hit a dead end at the moment"
"I'm sure you will crack it, little beats John Gammon" "Thanks for the faith in me Saron. Are you feeling nervous about this? I know I am" "A bit John. I guess you would like a boy, most men do" "To be honest as long as he or she is healthy that's all that matters"

They arrived at the class in room 201 at Jack Turners school in Dilley Dale. John could see all the men appeared out of place but the women slotted straight in. Halfway through they stopped for a coffee break and John got talking to a guy who played for Waggy at Rowksly. "So you know Waggy well

SERVED COLD

then?" "Yes, I've played at Rowksly for about four seasons now, I was originally at Micklock Town, played at a decent level then" "Sorry, I didn't get your name?" "Chris Raker" "Pleased to meet you Chris, I'm John Gammon" "Oh wow, you are that famous copper aren't you?" "Hardly famous mate, just do my job" Sandra Heckwhite who was taking the class asked everybody to go back through.

The class finished at 9.00pm and John took Saron back home. "That wasn't so bad was it John? I see you made a friend" "Yes, Chris is a nice lad" "His wife is Jane, you should go and watch Rowksly some weekends, it would take your mind off work John" "I think you may be

SERVED COLD

right Saron" "There isn't a class next week but there is one the following week, are you still coming?" "Of course, we are in this together" John wanted to ask her again if they could try and get back together but he didn't want a no answer so he left it.

The following day Gammon arrived at the station to more bad news, there had been another murder. The station was in pandemonium, apparently a high school teacher was taking some kids on a Duke of Edinburgh course and they found a body of a man by the side of the old outside toilets of the Black Bess in Biffin by Hittington.

"Two of the lads had sneaked into the old building intent on having a cigarette, I'm afraid

SERVED COLD

they got more than they
bargained for sir" "Ok Magic,
have you sent Wally?" "Yes and
DI Smarty has gone with DS
Bass" "Ok well I'd best get over
there" Gammon set off on one of
his favourite drives to the quaint
village of Biffin by Hittington. It
was almost 12.10pm when he
arrived and it was just as Steve
Condray and Phil Sterndale
pulled into the car park. "Hey
John, good to see you mate are
you stalking us or are you
buying us a pint?" "Sorry lads,
police business around the back,
before you ask Steve, no I can't
comment" Phil laughed, "He's
got the measure of you one pint"
and they disappeared through
the ornate village pub door
while Gammon went around the
back. Bass and Smarty were

SERVED COLD

talking to a farmer whose field
was adjacent to the pub.
"Bloody hell its John Gammon"
the man said, "not seen thee
since tha were knee high to a
grasshopper lad, how are you?"
"I'm good thanks Marvin how's
your Billy doing he went in the
air force didn't he?" "Yes but he
came out four year back, his
missus was fed up of the life,
they have a fish and chip shop
down in Suffolk where his lass
was from" "Give him my best
please Marvin" "Aye I will lad"
"We asked Mr Gill if he had
seen anything suspicious but he
said he didn't come over to this
field much this time of year so
couldn't help"
"Ok let me see what Wally has
for us" Gammon stuck his head
round Wally's white tent and got

SERVED COLD

the usual derisory comment and Wally came out. "What we got Wally?" "Not a lot yet, a male maybe late forties early fifties, his neck was broken and yes, he has a tattoo but other than that you will have to wait until the morning John" "Ok mate, 9.00am, don't forget" "Would I? it's etched into my soul John" and Wally laughed going back into the white tent. "Right Dave, you and Kate do the house to house, I know it's a sleepy village but they know if a stranger has been in their village, spend the day taking statements please. Have you spoke with the landlord and landlady yet?" "No not yet" "Ok I will do that then" "Well ain't that a surprise?" Smarty said and laughed. Gammon just smiled.

SERVED COLD

Steve Condray and Phil were still at the bar. "What you having John?" "Just a coke please Phil, that farmer guy that has the field next to the pub, is he local?" " Yeah, his grandad, his dad and now him farmed that John why?" "Oh just wondered" "So who is the body then?" "Well you know I can't say Phil even if I knew but it's too early, forensics are working on it. Look lads I need a quick word with the landlord and landlady so I'm going in the back. If you are here when I come back I will get you a drink" "No worries John, we are going now anyway, catch you in The Spinning Jenny" "Ok lads thanks" Gammon sat at the kitchen table at the back of the pub with Alf Richards and his wife Molly,

SERVED COLD

they had owned the Black Bess
for about twenty years John
thought.

"So, did either of you see
anything suspicious over the last
few days?" "Well there was a
guy in here two nights ago and I
said to Alf we best watch him,
he looked like trouble" "Oh
Molly you over react, he had a
swastika on his forehead Mr
Gammon and she hates tattoo's
does our Molly. He was a s good
as gold and left just after ten
pm" Gammon made a note that
again Baynes name had been
mentioned.

He headed back to the station
knowing tomorrow he would
have to go to somebody's family
and tell them the sad news. He
finished some paperwork and
decided enough was enough

SERVED COLD

Gammon called it a night and headed for a quick beer at the Spinning Jenny and hopefully a take –away from the pub.

The pub was busy, not many in John knew so he stood at the bar, Tracey Rodgers was working, she said Wez was cooking as Lindsay had a cold and was having the night off. He finished his first drink and was just ordering another when Jack Etchings came in. "What are you drinking Jack?" "I'll have a pint of Stella please old lad" "Where Shelley?" They were rarely seen apart. "Oh she is having one of girlie parties, I dunna know what they call them but the house is full of women until 11.00pm so I have come out of the way, Sheba Filey just dropped me off and she said she

SERVED COLD

would pick me up after the party" "That was good of her mate" "Yes she is a nice girl is Sheba. You could do a lot worse but I hear you have a baby on the way with Saron, are you two going to get back together?" "I would like to Jack but I'm not getting the vibe to be honest" "Dunna give up lad if that's what tha wants" "I think it is what I want to be honest" "Well I know me and Shelley have had our ups and downs but we are as much in love today as we were all those years ago when I met her at a dance in Micklock" "Yes mate, everybody can see that, to be honest we all say what a great couple you are" "Well like all things John you have to work at it so if Saron is what you want then I wish you the best of luck old lad"

"This looks an in-depth conversation you two" "Hey up Kev, what you doing here?"

"Doreen's down at that party thing the girls are having so it's brandies all round me thinks. Jack was about to say no but Tracey Rodgers had already dispensed three double brandies, the night carried on in the same vein, it was almost 12.30am and Wez had joined in so it was getting a bit crazy.

It was 1.00am when Sheba came for Jack with Doreen who wasn't too pleased to see Kev in such a state, Wez had already said John could stop so he declined Sheba's offer for a lift, John thought that was the best

SERVED COLD

route if he was too have any chance with Saron.

The following morning Wez shouted him to say his breakfast was ready. Lindsay still wasn't well so he had got up and done breakfast. "Very good of you mate, I'll have this and settle up with you then get off to work" "Don't be soft" said Wez in his Barnsley accent, "You are our guest mate" and he disappeared back to the kitchen.

Gammon arrive at work at 8.50am just enough time to get a cup of dishwater that supposedly passed for coffee from the machine then headed for the incident room.

By 9.00am the team were assembled. "Ok we have another body so over to you Wally" Wally stood up, Gammon smiled, he was wearing a pair of burgundy corduroys with a checked shirt and a brown gilet with his half-rimmed glasses perched precariously on the end of his nose, Gammon nudged him, "Your zips undone mate" Wally quickly arranged himself. There was no doubt Wally could be eccentric at times but he was the best forensic guy he had ever worked with.

"Ok everybody, sorry about that, the victim was male, we think in his mid- sixties, he was drugged, tattooed like the others then murdered before eventually being placed behind the Black Bess at Biffin by Hittington, we can't be sure of the time of death because the drug used slowed the heart to almost a standstill whilst he was tattooed with

SERVED COLD

B23318 on the left side of his chest" "Do we know who he is?" "Yes, his name is Maurice Gates, he has a fruit and veg shop in Biffin by Hittington, we have checked our records and he was off Polish descent. Mr Gates was mid –sixties" "Any sign of a struggle?" "Only some movement when the number was being tattooed." "The big question is, did you find any DNA?" "Sorry, whoever is doing this is very careful not to leave traces of DNA""" Ok thanks, great information" Gammon placed a picture of Maurice Gates with the others on the incident board. "That's four tattooed victims and one old lady, they are stacking up people, study each victim, look for connections, their pastimes

SERVED COLD

who they associated with there is something we are missing team. With it being Friday tomorrow, any of you that want to work the weekend on this do so and let's have a brain storming session on Monday at 9.00am, thanks" and Gammon closed the meeting.

He knew this case wasn't going well with just one real suspect and virtually nothing to go on it would not be long before questions will be asked of him and his team.

After the session he had the night before he decided to go straight home and check on DC the cat, as usual, the moment he walked through the door the cat was round his legs. Like we all do, John began talking to the cat, he knew in reality it wasn't

SERVED COLD

going to answer him back but
it's something all animal lovers
do.

John poured himself a large
Jameson's and popped one of
Phyllis Swan's homemade
lasagnes in the microwave,
without his trusted cleaner and, I
guess, carer, he would have been
lost he thought.

After finishing his meal he
grabbed a book from the shelf.
"Falling Leaves and Mountain
Ashes" by Brenda George, DS
Bass had said how good the
books were, she loved her
writings and had given John the
book some months earlier and
due to work commitments etc he
hadn't found the time to read it.
Based on North American
mountain folk John was soon
tucked up in bed with DC curled

SERVED COLD

by his side, he began reading page after page.

It was soon 12.30 am and with one hundred and thirty- six pages read he thought he had best get some sleep, the tattoo murders were taking a massive toll on everyone at Bixton and as much as he didn't want to put the book down he knew he had to get some sleep.

SERVED COLD

Chapter 5

The following morning John decided to take the route through Dumpling Dale, it was a pleasant Peak District morning, the old Manor house which stood high on top of Dumpling Dale shimmered with the sunlight behind it, all the wild flowers were out so in the distance it looked like a carpet of purple, yellow, red and green. This was a magical place John thought as he climbed the winding road that would eventually take him on the road to Bixton.

The old Manor House had stood empty since nineteen twenty- six and nobody locally knew who still owned it although quite a few people had asked around with a hope of purchasing it.

SERVED COLD

John eventually arrived at the station, had a quick check with PC Magic on the front desk on the night's events which had been largely uneventful, he grabbed a coffee and headed to his office fully intent on getting through his paperwork pile. He had only just sat down when the phone rang, it was the Assistant Chief Constable, Brian Martin. "Gammon we have a big problem, you have five murder victims, what the hell is happening? The press boys are all over us, also, the deputy prime minister has had Dorothy Lyngate from The Globe pestering him, she is somewhat of a spokesperson for the bloody tabloids, they want a televised briefing" Gammon tried to tell him that wasn't a good idea but he spoke over him. "It will be held at Northcliffe Hall just outside Derby at 2.00pm today, I want you and your head of forensics there and let me tell you, we had better have some answers" and the phone fell silent. Gammon went immediately to see Wally and told him the situation. "Bloody hell John, I said I would pick my brother up from hospital at 2.00pm, he has had a hernia operation" "Don't worry, get DI Smarty to do it for you, the Assistant Chief Constable wasn't impressed" "That's all well and good mate but we have nothing, we are going to look like clowns!" "I know, I tried to tell him but he just spoke over me, see you at 1.00pm Wally, I am sorry about this mate" Wally

SERVED COLD

walked away chuntering to himself at the injustice of it all. Gammon carried on with his paperwork then called in DS Bass, "How are you doing Kate?" "Just hitting a brick wall sir, I think even if they had information they either wouldn't share or the language barrier would hinder it" "Ok Kate, put it aside for now" "I don't mind to keep trying sir" "No, it was a long shot anyway"

Bass left Gammon with really no idea what he was going to say at the press conference. The more he thought about it the angrier he felt toward Brian Martin for not understanding. He shouldn't feel like this, he had dealings many times with the stupidity of the hierarchy

SERVED COLD

and he guessed that's why he was just a Detective Inspector. Wally was waiting with his parka fully buttoned up at the front desk. "Are you cold Wally? its quite nice outside" He just nodded, John wasn't sure if he was mad at him or seething with the situation, either way both of them were not in the right mood for a scrambling pack of media wolves he thought.

They arrived at the hall and Brian Martin met them, he was a stocky guy with brown hair clearly dyed as he must have been almost sixty John thought. "Right, I'm Brian Martin, which one of you is Gammon? You I hope" he said looking at Gammon and dismissing Wally with his Parka still fully

SERVED COLD

buttoned up, Gammon took an instant dislike to this pompous man. "Right, follow me" They entered the big hall where a stage had been set up the lights were bright from all the TV crews, Brain Martin led them to the stage, John felt he was a sacrificial lamb at some kind of ritual killing.

Wally was still not showing any interest. "Ok ladies and gentlemen of the press, we will take questions in the order we agreed" said the man sat next to Gammon who apparently was the police media spokesman. "If you could direct any questions at Detective Inspector John Gammon of Bixton police and the head of forensics John Walvin, also of Bixton police please, the Assistant Chief

SERVED COLD

Constable would prefer this as
these guys are working at the
coal face, so as to speak"
"DI Gammon, Steve Lewis Sky
News, how many suspects do
you have for the five murders?"
Gammon cleared his throat,
"One maybe two at this time"
"One maybe to DI Gammon? Is
it one or is it two?" "One that we
consider a likely suspect and
that we are watching closely, the
other we are not totally
convinced" "Bill Michaels BBC
News, Mr Walvin, have you
been able to find DNA on any
victims?" "That is a question I
will not answer for fear of
jeopardising the case" "I can
take that as a no then Mr
Walvin" "You may take it as
you please young Man" "Sarah
Thorne, ITV News, DI

SERVED COLD

Gammon, do you believe you are close to finding the killer?" "I believe we are getting close but you say killer, that is presumptuous, there may be more than one person involved" "So there are two?" "I didn't say that, what I meant was we have to keep an open mind at all times" "Yes Steve?" "DI Gammon why are the victims being tattooed?" "We are working on some possibilities and this could well be the killer's downfall" "So you think the tattoos are significant?" Gammon sighed he wished he hadn't said that. "We are taking all facets of the killings into account, yes Steve" "I have a question for Mr Walvin, you are head of forensics, how many years have you been doing the

SERVED COLD

job?" Gammon jumped in.
"What are you implying Mr
Lewis?" "Just that I get the
distinct impression that Mr
Walvin doesn't want to be here
today" "Ok Mr Lewis, you have
had your say, I won't have a
member of my team
compromised any longer, press
conference over" and Gammon
pulled off his mike and Wally
did the same leaving Martin
with the press boys ripping into
him, Gammon and Wally got in
their car and drove back to
Bixton. "Thanks John"
"Probably cost us our jobs or
demotion at the very least Wally
all because of that pompous
dick- head not listening"
Once back at Bixton PC Magic
said the phone hadn't stopped
ringing and DI Gammon was to

SERVED COLD

call Landon Benchoff at the Home office as soon as he got in, Magic gave Gammon the number, Gammon prepared himself, he was not going to take this lying down.

"John Gammon, Bixton Police"

"Oh good afternoon DI Gammon, thank you so much for calling me so promptly, I am guessing you are expecting reprisal because of what happened today at the press conference?" Gammon was just about to stand his corner when Benchoff laughed. "I just want to say well done to you and your colleague, we in the Home Office are well aware of the cuts that have taken place at Bixton and what a good job you are doing" It was clear Martin had a knee jerk reaction to some

SERVED COLD

media pals. "There will be no repercussions, I found it most enjoyable watching Martin squirming and not having a clue what to say so well done" The phone went dead. Gammon sat looking at Losehill completely shocked at the conversation he had just had, he phoned down to Wally and he was back to normal. "They never cease to amaze me John, thanks for letting me know"

It was almost 5.30pm and John was contemplating calling at the Tow'd Man to see Saron, he closed his office door locking it behind him and headed to see her. To his surprise she was sat at the bar with Paddy laughing and joking when he arrived, he wished he hadn't gone. He was beginning to think there was

SERVED COLD

more to their relationship than she was telling John or wanted him to know!!

He ordered a drink and asked them out of politeness if they wanted one. Saron said she was fine and after a bit of deliberation so did Paddy. John decided to stand at the end of the bar talking to Kathy Vickers, he was seething inside, it was as if she was wallowing in winding John up, he finished his drink, slipped to the toilet and left. Maybe she didn't want John and he had to accept it but why was he stepping on egg shells when she was blatantly flirting with Paddy? The old John Gammon needed to come back out he thought.

SERVED COLD

Once back home he settled back down with his book but fell asleep fifty pages in.

He decided to nip into work the next day with it being Saturday to see who from the team was in. When he arrived he asked Magic who had turned in, Magic said just DS Bass was in the office. What was wrong with his team? he was surprised. He entered DS Bass's office and she was busy tidying up so not really working on the tattoo case.

"Kate have you got a minute" "Yes sir" "Come to my office and get us both a coffee please" "Ok sir, just black no sugar?" "Yes please Kate" DS Bass was soon back with the coffees. "Sit down Kate, I want to ask you something" "Fire away sir" "I

SERVED COLD

am surprised there is only you in today" "Well, you know how things are." "Sorry Kate but no, I don't" "Look sir I'm not a snitch by any means" " Don't worry Kate, I'm not going to say you have said anything" "The guys are saying they are being asked all the time about the case and they don't feel we have any direction, you seem distant sir and they are not used to that with you" Gammon was a bit taken aback but maybe he was not quite on the ball with the Saron thing and the baby. "Ok Kate I appreciate your honesty, thank you. Please do not tell anyone we have had this conversation, I will put things right" "Ok sir" Gammon left the station and headed straight to the Spinning Jenny. "Wez, a week

SERVED COLD

today I want to throw a party"

"Anything special John?"

"Yeah, me getting my Mojo back" Wez laughed, "Any excuse for a party, I'm with you on that" "Free bar and I really want to push the boat out on the food, tell Lindsay no expense spared, put lobster on, in fact, anything, ask her to be really creative" "Will do John, how many are you catering for?" "Whoever is in the pub so if you work on ninety it should be about right do you reckon?" That will do nicely. Now can you get Tony on the Karaoke and disco?" "Should be ok mate" John was pleased that was sorted, he sent a text to all of his close friends and said there was a party at the Spinning Jenny the

SERVED COLD

following Saturday, just for the sake of having a party he put. John woke up the following day hoping his party idea would work he, decided to get back doing the things he liked doing like walking on a Sunday, his whole mind had been taken up with Saron and the baby and he was determined it was time out he needed. Saron either wanted the John Gammon she had loved once or not, it was no longer going to be the watered-down John he thought.

He laced his well- worn favourite walking boots, gave DC a stroke and said he would see her later, it was only 8.15 am but already it was a warm day. Roger Glazeback had just finished milking and walked

SERVED COLD

part of the way up the drive
where they parted.

John had decided to head for
Waterdale just outside of the
village of Pommie, there was a
nice little café on the way into
Pommie called Strangers
Welcome, Stranglers, as the
locals called it because of its
notoriety for massive portions,
had been in the same family for
one hundred and twenty years, it
had never closed, it was even
open through two World Wars.
John had two walk through two
dales before arriving just outside
Pommie and the famous
Stranglers. It was now 10.30am,
the café was busy but not
rammed so John got a place by
the window which overlooked
where he was walking to,

SERVED COLD

Waterdale. The sun was intense so John stripped down a couple of layers and rolled them up into his rucksack.

A lady in her late fifties arrived with a note-pad, "Can I get you a drink?" "Could I have a large strong black coffee please?" "You can, have you decided what you would like to eat sir?" "I'll take the Stranglers sandwich but no tomato please" "Ok so you want bacon, sausage, fried egg, mushrooms and Stranglers fried potato on a doorstep white?" "That would be great thank you"

He felt he was being a bit greedy but he was really hungry. The coffee and food arrived together and looking at the sandwich John thought maybe he had been a bit greedy, it was overflowing.

SERVED COLD

"Any sauce sir?" "Oh, um, brown please" the lady smiled in a way John knew she had seen this reaction many times over the years.

He finished his sandwich and felt ready to burst, he paid the lady giving her a generous tip. Outside the climb up to Waterdale looked daunting now but he set off, it would normally take him about fifteen minutes but after that sandwich it was closer to twenty-five when he reached the summit.

The view from the top was incredible, he sat for a while listening to some music on his phone, it was so peaceful, there was nobody about. He was just about to put his phone back in his rucksack when it rang.

"John, where are you?"

SERVED COLD

"Top of Waterdale just outside Pommie village Dave" "I have some bad news mate, DS Yap has been attacked, he is in intensive care in Bixton" "What the hell, do we know why Dave?" "No, I just got the call from Magic, he has been trying to ring you" "I would have been out of signal mate until I got up here. Can you pick me up in Pommie?" "Yes mate, where will you be?" "I'll wait by the Youth Hostel next to the village Chippy" "Ok mate, I will be half an hour" "DI Smarty rang off and John headed back down Waterdale to Pommie, they met almost at the same time and John got in the car.

"What do we think happened?" "I don't know yet mate, hoping DS Yap can tell us" Although it

SERVED COLD

was Sunday the hospital was very busy, John saw one of the nurses who told him they had to wait, Yap was in theatre, he had lost a lot of blood and she was afraid it was touch and go. Dave and John sat together, it was six hours later when a surgeon took them into a side room.

"Gentlemen I'm afraid your colleague didn't make it, he fought and fought but his loss of blood initially was the problem, I am very sorry" Smarty put his head in his hands. "Was he stabbed more than once?" "No DI Gammon, just the once but it went straight through his heart I'm afraid"

Gammon and Smarty left the hospital. "Where did he live Dave?" "He had just moved to Ackbourne with his wife Lucy"

SERVED COLD

"We'd best go and break the news, shit, I hate this part of the job. Get Wally, I want every inch of where he was stabbed in Derby going over, also the knife, I will get this piece of shit" Seventeen Lime Tree was a small detached house on a cul-de-sac, very neat and clearly a few people with money lived here. "Blimey Dave, how did he afford this?" "His wife is something to do with the Government, she worked in Parliament three days a week" John rang the doorbell and a pretty auburn- haired girl in her mid- thirties answered, "Lucy Yap?" "That's correct, how can I help you?" "I'm DI Gammon and this is DI Smarty, may we come in?" "What's the problem?" "I'm afraid Ian has

SERVED COLD

been fatally wounded in Derby sometime last night" "What? No, I spoke with him about 10.00pm" "Why was he in Derby?" "He wouldn't say, he never discussed his work but he said he would be home sometime today but may be out again tonight" Suddenly the shock hit Lucy and she started to cry Smarty comforted her. "Is there anybody we can call who could sit with you?" "My sister lives next door but one" "Do you want somebody from the police to come over?" "No I will be fine" "I'm sorry but you will need to identify Ian Lucy" "When?" "Tomorrow if that's ok, we can send a car" "No, it's fine, me and my sister will drive over but thank you" Lucy's sister arrived, as Gammon and

SERVED COLD

Smarty couldn't do anymore
they left her to grieve.
"How the hell did this happen? I
wasn't aware he was working on
anything Dave" "No I wasn't
John" "Who was his best friend
at the station?" "Well he tended
to spend a lot of time with DI
Lee but not sure you would say
they were mates" "Ok we'll look
tomorrow, let's get DI Lee and
see if he can shed any light on
what Ian was working on.
Let's get over to Derby, call
Magic and get the address"
"John Magic is now saying he
was found staggering in front of
Ackbourne Town Hall, it
appears he was stabbed around
the back of the building" "How
the bloody hell did we go from
Derby to Ackbourne? bloody
useless" Dave didn't comment,

SERVED COLD

he could see John was upset at losing one of his officers.

They arrived at Ackbourne which was a busy tourist location on a Sunday, there was blood on the steps of the Town Hall and a trail leading around the back where Wally had set up the incident tent.

"What you got Wally?" "Not a lot John, we do have half a foot print, it appears that DS Yap knew his assailant, lots of blood but until I get the body this afternoon I won't know for sure" "Ok, 9,00 am tomorrow, I need answers quick on this Wally, he is one of ours" "I will do my best mate" "Drop me back home please Dave and you get back to your family" "Ok John, you don't want a quick drink, might help you relax a

SERVED COLD

bit?" It was unusual for Dave
Smarty to go for a drink so John
accepted. They called at the
Wop and Take at Trissington,
John ordered two pints and two
brandies, he raised his glass, "To
DS Yap, a bloody good copper,
we will get who did this mate"
John said looking to the
heavens. Both men were upset
and the brandies were flowing, it
was almost 11.00pm when Dave
Smarty's phone rang. "Sorry
sweetheart, just having a drink
with John. Are you sure you
don't mind? Ok thank you, we
are at the Wop and Take at
Trissington" "Janet is going to
fetch us and take you home,
could you pick me up in the
morning so I can get the car
from here John" "Yes of course
mate, will be nice to meet your

SERVED COLD

wife" "Not sure on that one mate, I mean its 11.00pm on a Sunday night" they both laughed.

"How are you and Saron this pub is on her Mums estates isn't it?" "Yes, I'm not sure about me and Saron, look Dave, don't repeat this but Saron is having my baby" "Wow well done mate" "It would be great but I get the impression she is giving me the run-around, I went up to see her last night and she was sat with that Irish guy who is working at Pippa's Frozen Foods at Lingcliffe, she was sat at the bar laughing and joking with him and hardly had the time of day for me mate, that's why I have been a bit distant but next Saturday I am throwing a party at the Spinning Jenny for

SERVED COLD

everyone at work and a load of friend's, free bar and some real nice food so you must bring Janet, it's my way of making it up to the team" "John you didn't have to do that" "I do Dave, I have neglected the team because of things in my private life and I have never done that before so trust me, the old John Gammon is back, whatever the consequences mate"

Just then a slim lady in her late forties John thought, came over. "Come on then Dave, introduce me" "This is my boss, John Gammon Janet" "Well, technically that isn't correct, we are the same rank Dave" "Yeah but we all see you as the boss" "So this is the famous John Gammon, very nice to meet you at last, I have heard a lot about

SERVED COLD

you" "All good I hope"
"Mostly" she said with a cheeky
grin. "So, are you boys ready?"
"This is very good of you Janet,
guess it hit us both harder than
we thought with DS Yap dying
like that"
Janet drove him back and he told
Dave he would pick him up at
8.00 am in the morning.
John went straight go bed but
struggled to get too sleep he
kept going over and over in his
mind why would Ian Yapp be at
the Ackbourne Town Hall the
exact place of the Jewish
Community and their meetings,
was he meeting whoever killed
him on the pretence that the
assailant had information? Why
would he not come to me John
thought. Was this thing with
Saron deeper than he had

SERVED COLD

thought, had he not given DS Yap the time he might have needed? He had a terrible night's sleep and he felt quite dreadful as he picked up DI Smarty who, to be fair, didn't look a lot better. He dropped Smarty off for his car and carried on into work. The weather was a bit like John's mood, drizzly, damp and wet. He arrived at 9.00am ready for the meeting, the incident room was full, Gammon could sense the feeling of all present on receiving the news that a colleague had been murdered. "Ok everyone, you are all aware I am sure, of the news we got last night about our friend, our colleague and a damn good copper. I believe Ian was working on something to do

SERVED COLD

with the case, did any of you have any conversations with Ian, anything that might lead to his killer?"

DI Lee stood up. "As you know, Ian and myself were good friends, he so wanted to be a Detective Inspector, we spoke about this many times over the last year, all I know is he said one of his informants had given him a tip off about the case. I did ask him what and he joked with me that this was his hour and he said you would be impressed"

"So, Ian had some news on the case or he thought he did, I am guessing our killer got wind of this and met Ian on the pretence of giving him information, I think he murdered him because he knew something.

SERVED COLD

There is a massive connection going on here with the Jewish community, we have to put our heart and soul into finding what it is. Wally any evidence?" Wally stood up clearly shaken at the loss of DS Yap. "Whoever stabbed him he struggled with, we have DNA from under Ian's nails" "Do we have a match?" "Yes, Marty Baynes" "That scumbag, DS Smarty and DI Lee go over and arrest him, get him a solicitor, don't interview him until I get back from seeing Maurice Gates' wife, have you got the address DS Bass?" "Yes sir" "Ok, we will give the lady the bad news. Guys I know we are all upset about DS Yap but no rough stuff with Baynes, we have enough on with the media on our case currently"

SERVED COLD

Lee and Smarty went off to arrest Baynes and Gammon and Bass set off to see Mrs Gates who lived at Wyncote, a village about four miles from Biffin by Hartington.

Gates had lived in a really nice house overlooking a stream, the detached former barn conversion was quite impressive, there must have been money in fruit and veg Gammon thought. As they walked up the drive a woman in her late forties stopped them. "Can I help you?" "We are looking for Mrs Gates" they showed their warrant cards. "Oh, she is in the house, she hasn't been well lately so I am over from Canada to keep an eye on her, dad was meeting some friends at The Black Bess, it was Wyncote's annual fishing holiday so he was meeting his mates and they will be back on Sunday"

"Could we go up to the house please Miss Gates?" "Oh, I'm married, my name is Olivia Kulim, I married a Canadian twenty -three year ago Mr Gammon" They stepped into the house, a frail older lady greeted them, Olivia explained that Gammon was here to talk to them.

"There is no easy way to say this but I'm afraid your husband has been found dead behind the Black Bess public house in Biffin by Hittington" Unknown to Gammon Mrs Gates showed signs of Alzheimer's but Olivia understood what he had said, with tears rolling down her cheek she said, "How can this be

SERVED COLD

Mr Gammon?" "I honestly don't
know at this time, could we go
in another room?" "Yes of
course, I'm afraid mum doesn't
understand"

"You said your father was going
on a fishing trip, is that correct?"
"Well, that's what he told me"
"Was it an annual thing?"
"Apparently, up until this year
mum was ok but there was no
way she could be on her own
this year and I didn't want dad
to miss out, he is a hardworking
man Mr Gammon, sorry, was a
hardworking man" "This might
seem like a silly question but
was your father born here?"
"Yes, but my grandparents were
Polish Jews and suffered terribly
during the war, my grandad
survived Auschwitz but his wife
wasn't so lucky" "How old was

your father Olivia?" "He would have been sixty -seven at the end of this month. After the war grandad made his way to the UK, they told him he could go back to Poland but he feared the Nazi's could rise again so he came here and made his home" "Interesting, so your grandad was in a concentration camp, this might seem like a silly question but did your grandfather or perhaps your dad change the family name?" "I don't think so and to be honest grandad didn't have any possessions when he came here so who knows?" "Sorry to have to ask you this but the body of your father will need identifying at the morgue tomorrow at 11.00 am, could you do that?" "Yes of course" "Would you like

SERVED COLD

somebody from grief
counselling to come over?" "No,
I will be fine, it's perhaps good
mum doesn't understand Mr
Gammon" "Do you have
transport?" "Yes I have a hire
car but thank you anyway"
"Just one other thing, would you
know if your father was a
member of any local Jewish
societies?" "I honestly don't
know, he wouldn't talk about
grandad and the war" "Ok Olivia,
we will leave you in peace"

SERVED COLD

Chapter 6

Gammon and Bass set off back to the station and the interview with Marty Baynes. Magic said they were all in interview room one. Gammon instructed DS Bass to see if Maurice Gates was a member of the Jewish Survivors Club in Ackbourne while he interviewed Baynes with Smarty and DI Lee.

Gammon entered the room and DI Lee introduced everyone to the tape. "Mr Baynes, we meet again" Baynes sat with his arms folded just staring menacingly at Gammon and Smarty. "Let's start by asking you where you were on Monday night between the hours of 6.30pm and midnight?" "Home" Baynes said in an arrogant way.

SERVED COLD

"Tell me something, this obsession with the Nazi party, what is your take on these killings?" "No comment" "You see Mr Baynes, during our investigations your name keeps cropping up?" "Really? I must be a popular guy Mr Gammon, are you jealous?" At this point Gammon put his hand on Smarty's knee.

"Were you in the vicinity of Ackbourne town hall on Sunday night?" "What are you trying to pin on me, the murder of that copper?"

We have your DNA from skin traces found under DS Yap's finger nails, how do you explain that. Mr Baynes?" Baynes whispered into his solicitor's ear. "My client wishes to tell

you something but there is to be
no prejudice against him"
"Let's hear what he has to say"
"Look, you know I am member
of HRP33 well, so was DS Yap,
he was recruited about three
months ago" "Don't try to
wriggle out of this Baynes by
blaming DS Yap" "Ask
headquarters to look at the
books, he called himself Ian
Boff so you lot wouldn't know"
"We will take a break here"
Gammon told Smarty to get DS
Bass to check this out quickly.
Gammon went back and carried
on with the interview. "So you
want to me to believe on of my
officers was in your hatred
party?" "Believe what you want
but it's the truth, I got to know
him real well, he said he was

SERVED COLD

sick of this government and the Jews holding all the money" Smarty came back and whispered in Gammons ear that it was in fact correct, there was an Ian Boff registered, he also said that his wife's maiden name was Boff so in all likeliness Ian Yap and Ian Boff were one and the same.

"Ok Mr Baynes, let's say you are telling the truth, it still doesn't alter the fact that DS Yap had your DNA under his finger nails" "Look, I had arranged to meet him down the alley at the side of the Town Hall, when I got there he had already been stabbed, I tried to help him but he was in so much pain he dug his nails into me, I had to go because I knew you lot

SERVED COLD

would not believe me" "So you left Ian Yap to bleed to death? I don't believe you Mr Baynes. I think DS Yap was onto something about the murders in the Jewish community and I believe you were involved" Baynes turned to his solicitor. "See I told you they wouldn't believe me, they are trying to hang this on me because of my connection with the far left" "Mr Baynes I am going to hold you for twenty fours in that time we will do a complete search on your house and vehicle, depending on what that throw's up we will decide if you are to be charged, do I make myself clear?" Baynes nodded. "Take him to the holding cell DI Smarty please"

SERVED COLD

Gammon got DS Bass and Simon Colley, who was the Police Federation representative, he wanted to check DS Yap's locker. Gammon took Yap's note book but other than that there was very little, a couple of pictures of him and his wife and that was about it.

Gammon went back to his office and to his pure delight he found what he wanted further back in his notes, he had put "Joined HRP 3, hate what they stand for but if I can get close and get somebodies trust in this evil organisation then I'm sure I can crack this case" John felt elated that he didn't have a copper under his command that was a member of the far left but he felt somewhat guilty that Yap felt he

SERVED COLD

had to go off piste to try and climb the ladder in his career. Gammon called Wally and asked him to get a forensic team over to Baynes house, he also instructed DI Lee and DS Bass to go with three uniformed lads to do a total search, he had the car impounded as well.

It must be Baynes he thought. DI Smarty put his head around the door. "I hate that piece of shit John" "Read this" and he passed Yap's notebook to him. "I am so glad, I always liked Yap and when Baynes was spouting that crap I couldn't believe it. Question is did Baynes kill him John?" "At the moment it's a bit flimsy but hopefully the lads and Wally will find something incriminating" "Fingers crossed

SERVED COLD

John, oh by the way, Janet fell
for your charm mate, we will
both be there Saturday night, she
is really looking forward to it
and that really surprised me"
"Good, it should be a good night
just a shame about DS Yap but
we will also make it a
celebration of his life mate"
Gammon had to inform the
Chief Constable about DS Yap,
he explained the situation and
what he had found in his
notebook. The Chief was ok
with that but he said if by the
time is funeral is sorted there is
any shadow hanging over the
force then it won't be a force
funeral. Gammon agreed but he
was quite certain he was on
good ground so he had every
intention of ignoring the Chief
Constable with regard to the

SERVED COLD

funeral because there was no way one of his officers who had risked and given up his life for his job was going to his grave without full honours from the station.

Gammon rang Lucy Yap and explained what he would like to do and she said she would be very proud, she also asked him if he would say a few words at the Service. Apparently the funeral was to be a fortnight on Monday at Derby Crematorium. Gammon said unless she objected, his colleagues would carry him in to the crematorium. Lucy was really pleased with John's suggestion. "Ok Lucy, let me know a couple of days before the funeral and I will make the necessary arrangements, do you need

SERVED COLD

anything?" "No, I'm fine Mr Gammon" "Well you have my number, call me day or night if you want anything, we are all here for you" "Thank you for those kind words, it is very thoughtful of you"

Gammon decided it was time to call it a night, hopefully tomorrow there would be some good news on the Baynes house search. He decided to call at the Spinning Jenny for a take away. It was quite a pleasant night as he drove over from Bixton, his mind wandered to Saron, what was she playing at? this surely can't still be what happened over the wedding, he knew he was wrong but now they had a baby to consider in a few months and it wasn't just about the two of them anymore. He

SERVED COLD

arrived at the pub and parked at the back carpark walking down the old well-worn stone steps to the front of the pub.

He walked in and Tracey Rodgers was behind the bar. "Is Lindsay cooking tonight?" "No they have gone out with her sister, she has sold her house and has moved down here to open the wine bar and bistro "Dog House" in the village" "Oh crap, I wanted a take away" "Well if its food you want Carol Lestar is taking me off at 9.00pm and I have a fish pie that will easily feed two of us if you fancy coming back?" "Are you sure Tracey?" "I wouldn't have asked if I didn't want to" "Well that's great, thank you" John thought, what the hell, he was determined to stop thinking

SERVED COLD

about the Saron situation and start thinking about himself. Tracey got off at 9.00pm and John ordered a bottle of champagne to take with them as a thank you. They pulled up at the former stable block and it felt a bit eerie now knowing Jo and Steve's little one died in the fire just up the driveway. Tracey served up the fish pie with salad and they sat talking. "How long will you stay here Tracey?" "Steve signed the house over to me last week, he said it's what Jo would have wanted. I think the land is going to auction in about a month. He has moved on John which is nice for him, he is with India now" "Are you ok with that?" "Of course, she is kind of my sister although I don't know her really well. It's

SERVED COLD

amazing how much her and Jo are alike though John don't you think?" "I agree"

Tracey got up and put some music on, it was clearly her intention that was John was staying the night. It wasn't long before they were in a passionate embrace which lasted for almost an hour before both fell silent on the mat in front of the log burner. "Wow Mr Gammon, where did all that passion come from?" Although John felt like he had exorcised is demons he still didn't feel good about it. Without doubt the Saron thing was going away quickly. Tracey cuddled into John and they slept there all might. The following morning John left at six to go home and make sure DC was ok and showered ready for work.

SERVED COLD

With everything sorted he headed for the station hoping for some good news on the case. Everybody was already in the Incident room when Gammon arrived. "Ok, listen up everybody, we have Marty Baynes in custody, I need a result from yesterday's house search, Wally you go first please" "We turned the house upside down, we found no trace of any DNA other than Marty Baynes and his former girlfriend who was murdered, Ruth Weisner, the same DNA was in his car" "Thanks Wally but that isn't helping us, he was seeing Ruth Weisner so you would expect her DNA in his house and car. Anybody else got anything? Yes DS Bass" "Victim number two, I have

SERVED COLD

found Josef Guran's tattoo
which was B2008 that was used
on Herschel Sparks. Guran's
mother's maiden name was
Sparks!! Now either that is a
coincidence or we have some
kind of bizarre revenge going on
here"

"Brilliant work Kate, any luck
with the others?" "Nothing on
the first victim, it takes ages
because names were changed
and records have been lost but I
am working on victim number
three now"

"That is impressive work, well
done. Ok everybody, can we
think why the tattoo of Herschel
Sparks found its way onto Josef
Guran now we know his
mother's maiden name was
Sparks?" "Yes, DI Smarty" "My
guess is there was collaboration

SERVED COLD

with the Germans by Sparks."
"Good point but if that is the
case and Marty Baynes is our
killer what would his gripe be?"
"Not sure, I think we need to
look at all the members of the
Jewish Survivors Club in
Ackbourne" "That's a big task
DI Milton but seeing that you
volunteered I appreciate that, go
through all the names, find out
their parents' names even grand
-parents' names. DI Lee you
help Carl on this please"
"Ok, we'll give it a few days and
see what Carl, Kate and Peter
can come up with. Thanks
everyone"
Gammon left the meeting
feeling they were on the brink of
a breakthrough thanks to the
initiative of DS Bass. Magic
collared him. "Sir would it be

SERVED COLD

possible to have a word in your office" "Ok Magic, can we say 2.00pm tomorrow?" "Yes that's fine sir, is it ok to get one of the beat lads to watch the front desk?" "Yes of course" Gammon went back to his office, with DI Smarty's take on the case ringing in his ears maybe there was a tie up but what about Baynes? With nothing incriminating he had to let him go or apply for a holding extension but on what grounds? That was it, there was no choice, much as he felt he had something to do with the murders he had to let him go. He instructed Magic to speak with Baynes lawyer and release him. The following day Gammon made sure the team knew about the night all paid for at the

SERVED COLD

Spinning Jenny, he also called
Rita and Tony, Jack and Shelley,
Bob and Cheryl, Sheba Filey,
Tracey Rodgers, Steve and
India, Kev and Doreen, Phil and
Linda, Carol Lestar and Jimmy
Lowcee and a few others, he
was determined to have a good
night. He hadn't asked Saron on
purpose but he did ask Donna
Fringe knowing that the word
would get out.

Sure enough an hour after
asking Donna Saron called John.
"What's the problem John?"
"Problem, what problem?"
"Well you have invited all of our
friends to the party you are
throwing but you haven't asked
me"
"Look Saron, I called the other
night to see you, you could
hardly speak to me, you were sat

SERVED COLD

with Paddy laughing and joking
to the point that I felt
uncomfortable so I left" "Oh, so
it's the jealousy thing is it?" "No
it's not, you are carrying our
baby and to be real honest I
thought this would be our time
to get back together" "What,
because we are having a baby?
Are you saying that would
change the real John Gammon
because I don't think so in fact, I
know it won't, I was told you
went to Tracey Rodgers house
the other night and my bet is you
stayed over, so don't give me
crap about talking to somebody
at a bar, that is just hypocritical"
and she slammed the phone
down.

At least John knew where he
stood now. Poor Magic came to
see him at totally the wrong time

SERVED COLD

when he knocked on his door. "Come in" Gammon said in a hurried manner. "Afternoon sir, you said I could see you at 2.00pm today" "Oh yes Magic, what is it?" "Well I hope this doesn't seem to be jumping into a dead man's shoes but I wondered if I could come back on the team sir" Gammon didn't hesitate with his answer. "No, I think we need at least a DS or even a DI with the workload we have now Magic. Is that all?" Magic nodded clearly surprised at Gammon's brusque attitude. The problem was Saron had managed to get to him again because the real John Gammon would not have been so dismissive before. He did a bit more paperwork when Lucy Yap called to say the funeral was the

SERVED COLD

following Wednesday at 1.30pm at Derby Crematorium, she said the undertaker would get Ian's coffin in the hearse if his colleagues would carry him into the crematorium. John said that would not be a problem, she told him that the wake would be at the Wobbly Man in Toad Holes afterwards and all were welcome. Gammon thanked her and said he would be given a full police funeral.

Gammon felt annoyed that they had all these murders but still nobody in the frame, having now let Marty Baynes go he instructed two beat lads to do some surveillance on Baynes, nothing was sitting right with Gammon, his bloody private life was a mess, any chance with Saron looked like fading away

SERVED COLD

work wasn't going so well
either. What a mess he thought
as he stood looking across at
Losehill from his office picture
window. Unknown to Gammon
his day was about to get worse.
Magic called and said there was
a man and woman in reception
who said they had found a body.
"On my way Magic"
The man and woman were by
the front desk, the woman
looked dreadful and the man not
a lot better. "Come with me"
and Gammon took them into
interview room two and ordered
two teas for them, he told Magic
to get DI Smarty to come in as
well.
"I'm DI Gammon and this is my
colleague DI Smarty, how can
we help you?" The poor woman
was trembling and could hardly

SERVED COLD

speak and the man wasn't much better but he tried. "We stopped to have a little picnic at Puddle Dale, we dropped on this beautiful village with its duck pond and stocks just by chance, we quite often ride around the Peak District in the car, the wife isn't great on her feet. We tend to stop at some place with a view but today we decided to stop at this village, I walked over to the quaint cheese shop and ordered two sausage rolls and two cheese and Puddle Dale chutney sandwiches, I asked the lady if she had a toilet, she said they didn't but just up the lane from the duck pond there were some public toilets. It wasn't particularly for me it was for Amelia so when I got back I walked up with her, she went in

SERVED COLD

and let out an almighty scream. I probably shouldn't have but I rushed in, propped up on one of the toilets was a body, at first because it was decomposed, I couldn't tell if it was a woman or a man but it was a man" "A decomposed body? Just a minute, Dave get Milton and Lee with Wally and his team over to Puddle Dale.

Ok, I'd better take your names and addresses" "I'm Paul Wright and this is my wife Amelia Wright, we live at 14 Whitworth Terrace, Dilley Hillside in Dilley Dale, we moved here fourteen years ago with my job but we both retired last year" "Ok David, did you see anybody in the area?" "Not at first but when Amelia screamed there is a little house about eighty

SERVED COLD

metres away and the lady was watering her hanging baskets, she has stayed with the body"

"Ok well look, you have both had a terrible shock, I have your names and address if I need to speak with you again, here is my card if you need to contact me, we will take it from here, I'm very sorry for your shock"

Mr and Mrs Wright left and Gammon headed for Puddle Dale, the drive there was beautiful although John knew his arrival would be anything but.

He parked his car by the village pond and walked up the lane, he noticed the name of the lane leading to the public toilets was called Terrifying Row, he remembered they did a thing on it when he was at school. There

SERVED COLD

had been a row of house either side of the track road that had long since gone, it was reputed that eighteen people were murdered in the row over a seventeen-month period and the killer was never found, it felt a bit like that now he thought as walked up to the toilet.

Smarty was stood talking to a woman. Gammon flashed his warrant card. "You are?" "Sarah Muggins, I live at that cottage up there, I was watering my hanging basket when I heard the lady scream" "Sarah I am struggling to see how a body can virtually rot away and nobody notice, do the council clean the toilets?" "They are supposed to but I never see anybody. These toilets are hidden away I am surprised they are still open nobody uses them" "Clearly or we would not have a body rotting away. Have you seen anybody suspicious over the last three months?" I've only just got back from Australia, my son Jimmy lives out there and he asked me over for three months, I only got back four days ago. It's very quiet up here, never see a soul. My boy wants me to move over to him but I'm the wrong age for such a big upheaval" "Ok Sarah, thanks for your time, this is my card, if you think of anything please don't hesitate to contact me any time day or night" "I will Mr Gammon" and she wandered back up the lane.

Gammon sent Smarty and Lee back to the station, he had two beat guys watching the scene.

SERVED COLD

"What have we got Wally?" "A bloody mess John, that's what we have here" "Any early signs?" "Male and yes tattooed, we are fingerprinting and dusting everything down" Gammon felt almost sick from the stench.

"Wally try and get me something for the morning meeting at 9.00amplease" "This is going to be difficult John but I will do my best" "Good man" Gammon left to get some fresh air, he was walking back to the car when he noticed what looked like Marty Baynes coming out of the Cheese factory shop. "Mr Baynes, Mr Baynes?" "Now what? Can't you lot leave me alone, what's the problem now?" "It just seems odd to me that you have been in the

SERVED COLD

vicinity of previous murders and now this" "What? I'm shopping for cheddar and you think I'm spying on you? Get a life Gammon" Gammon went up close to him. "Let me tell you something off the record, I know you have an involvement in these murders you bloody sick individual and I aim to prove it" "Piss off, this is harassment, you will be hearing from my lawyer" and he smiled at Gammon. Gammon wanted to give him a serious slap but that wouldn't help things.

SERVED COLD

Chapter 7

It was two days before Wally could give Gammon anything from the body, after intensive forensics they had the name of the man murdered, it was a Bernard Dyan. DS Bass found he had lived in sheltered accommodation in Ackbourne he lived alone with no known relatives. His tattoo was B33101, he was of Polish/Jewish descent. Gammon contacted Abigail to see if she would meet him to discuss if she knew the murdered man, they arranged to meet in Ackbourne at the Clotted Cream café in the Market Square. It was 2.00pm and Gammon arrived and ordered a strong black coffee, he had just started to order when Abigail Harrop

SERVED COLD

arrived and ordered a Coca Cola, they both had a scone with jam and cream.

"So what's this about Mr Gammon, can I help you in anyway?" "We have another murder on our hands, this time the man was probably dead for at least three months. His name was Bernard Dyan, I wondered if he was somebody you may have come across at the Jewish Survivors meetings?" "Oh dear, yes I knew Bernard or Harpo as they older guys called him" "Harpo?" "Sorry, yes Harpo Marx because he hardly spoke, the Marx Brothers were before my time Mr Gammon" "And mine Abigail"

"Harpo was a nice guy, wouldn't hurt a fly, he came to every meeting, I guess I hadn't seen

SERVED COLD

him for a while but he was that
quiet I guess he wasn't missed,
how sad is that? Did you say he
had been murdered?" "Yes I'm
afraid so and it looks like it
could have been the first murder
because of the time he was left
to decompose and I'm afraid rats
had taken their toll also on the
poor man" "How dreadful Mr
Gammon, poor Harpo" "Do you
know any history about him,
how he got to be here in
England?" "No Mr Gammon,
like I said he was so quiet and
he didn't really mix, he just
wasn't a people person I guess"
"Ok Abigail, thank you for your
help, we will catch the person
responsible" "I really hope so,
there is a lot of fear at the
meetings but then again these
people know about fear even if

SERVED COLD

it's from their grandparents or
parents who lived through the
war Mr Gammon" "Yes they
have been persecuted Abigail,
Anyway, thanks for your help"
"Any time Mr Gammon"
Gammon left and headed
straight to the Spinning Jenny, it
was his party on Saturday and
he had Ian Yap's funeral
tomorrow.

John arrived at the Spinning
Jenny and to his surprise Sheba
was behind the bar. "Wow what
are you doing behind the bar?"
"My first night, never done it
before John but I am going to
Australia next year to see my
aunty and uncle so need the
extra cash. I was talking to
Lindsay and mentioned about
probably getting a little job at
night and she said I could work

SERVED COLD

here if I wanted so it's ideal"
"Well it will certainly drag the lads in having a good looking girl like you behind the bar" "Give over Gammon you smooth merchant" and she flashed her pearl white teeth and flicked her long dark hair as she walked down the bar to serve another customer. When she came back she thanked John for the invite on Saturday night then mentioned that Lucy Yap had asked if she would be going to the funeral. "I didn't know Ian too well but I know Lucy, we were on the Hittington Wakes committee together, lovely girl John" "Ok, well I will see you tomorrow as well then" "Happy days" she said giving John that seductive smile.

SERVED COLD

He was only going to stop for one but seeing Sheba behind the bar changed his mind. Before he knew it, the last drink was 11.20pm, Sheba offered him a lift home and John decided that faint heart never won fair lady so he asked her to stop and bring him back for his car in the morning, to John' surprise she said she would. They arrived at John's cottage and little DC melted Sheba's heart. "You never said you had a cat" "Let me introduce DC, this is the lovely Sheba" "DC, what does that stand for?" "Dark Chocolate!!" "But the cats pure white" "Yep!" and he laughed. "You get worse John Gammon" "You go upstairs and I'll bring us a drink up" John arrived with the drinks, Sheba was sat on the

SERVED COLD

end of the bed stroking DC who
had quite taken to her.

She had on a denim skirt with a
white blouse she was wearing
off her shoulders with a big pair
of earnings and the jet -black
hair, she looked how Hollywood
always portrayed a gypsy girl in
the movies. John put the cups on
the side and kissed her, she
responded and the embrace was
full on, her silky pure white skin
rubbing against John, this
somehow felt right, Sheba was a
very pretty girl with the figure of
a model and maybe this was
John Gammon at his best again.
They made love for almost an
hour, finally they lay on the bed.
"John do you remember the first
time we spent the night together
and I wouldn't let you make
love to me?" "How could I

SERVED COLD

forget? I think it scarred me for life" "Be quiet Gammon" and she play slapped him. "I'm not looking for a full-on relationship, I really enjoy your company and if you want it would be nice if we did things together until perhaps we both feel comfortable with together" "That's fine by me Sheba" Soon they were both asleep. The following morning Sheba was up and made John a bacon sandwich before dropping him off for his car at the Spinning Jenny. "See you this afternoon" she said. John kissed her full on and it felt good.

Gammon returned to work knowing that it would be tomorrow before Wally could give him a full report on the decomposed body, he finished

SERVED COLD

clearing his paperwork at the station and headed for the crematorium, they planned to be there for 1.00pm with Yap's coffin arriving at 1.30pm. John had decided he would speak some words but wanted it to come from the heart not something scripted.

The officers carrying the coffin were John, Dave Smarty, PC Magic had arranged for Di Trimble to cover him then there was DI Peter Lee, DI Carl Milton and DS John Winnipeg who had left some time ago to live in Liverpool with his girlfriend but said he was coming back because him and Yap had been friends when they worked together.

It was 1.20pm when the Chief Constable arrived and he made

straight to Gammon and pulled him aside. "DI Gammon, nothing is likely to embarrass the force in any way is there?" "No sir" "Good Gammon, great news, I can't stay for the wake, only here for the service I'm afraid" Typical Gammon thought. "Are you doing a reading?" "Yes sir" "Great, good man"

The hearse arrived and the officers put the coffin on their shoulders, the beat men did a guard of honour as they entered the crematorium.

His wife had chosen Islands in the Stream by Dolly Parton, apparently one of their favourite songs. They laid the coffin on the rollers then all sat down, Lucy Yap was being comforted by DS Bass on the front row.

SERVED COLD

The vicar, a man in his early forties stood at the front. "Dearly beloved, we are gathered here today to celebrate the life of not only an outstanding police officer but a husband to Lucy and friend to many of you in the congregation today, Ian Yap was a giant of a man, a man with principles and respect for others.

I would like you all to stand for our first hymn, There is a green hill far away" The congregation stood with DI Lee leading the singing, he was a church regular and had sung in the choir for many years. At the end of the hymn the vicar announced that John Gammon would now speak on behalf of Bixton Police.

SERVED COLD

John walked to the small wooden pulpit. He cleared his throat and began.

"Ian Yap, friend, colleague and a caring honest person. Ian was promoted under me to a detective sergeant and I remember the day very well and his excitement that he was going forward in his career.

Ian was a laid -back guy, I never saw him get angry or frustrated, he handled the public very well and I knew I could rely on him. Ian would have made a detective inspector within the next two years, there was no doubt about that. His untimely death, we believe, was that he had seen something on the current murder case sweeping the Peak District, I can assure Lucy, his dear wife there will be no stone left

SERVED COLD

unturned in our endeavours to
catch our friend and colleagues'
murderer.

Let me talk about Ian and his
obsession with his beloved
Derby County. I remember one
time working a case with Ian
and he asked if he could leave
spot on 5.00pm as Derby had an
FA Cup game at home and he
liked to be in his seat a good two
hours before kick- off, just to
savour the atmosphere. I played
with him a bit telling him I
would give him an answer later
on that day. It was 4.30pm and I
knew he was getting desperate,
eventually at 4.50pm he asked
again and I said ok, I always was
going to say yes, I just wanted
him to sweat a bit. The
following day I was driving to
work listening to Talk Sport and

SERVED COLD

they said Derby had been hammered eight nil and the manager Garth Sutton had been sacked, I couldn't wait to get to work to give Ian some stick about the manager and the score line. We had arranged to meet in Hittington at a small café to discuss the days stake out, when I got there Ian had ordered a strong black coffee for me and the sugariest cake you can imagine. He sat with a smirk on his face so I started "what was the score last night Ian?" "Eight one sir" "Oh, Derby won then?" "No sir, we lost" "Blimey, a tea bag stay's in the cup longer than Derby County did in the FA Cup!" "Thing is sir, it's only a Mickey Mouse Cup and it did us a favour, they sacked Sutton" I had to laugh as I bit into the

SERVED COLD

cake so I then asked him why the sugary cake? He laughed again "Thought you might give me some stick so I thought I would sweeten you up sir!" That was Ian, nothing fazed him. Good luck on your journey my friend" John left the pulpit, the mourners all clapped, the women were in tears, he noticed Sheba Filey was crying but he hadn't noticed Saron at the back of the room, she had worked with Ian Yap only for a short time but she made the effort with Donna Fringe to attend his funeral.

The vicar stood up. "I would now like to read a passage to you from John, chapter 14 verses 1-6

Do not let your hearts be troubled.

SERVED COLD

Trust in God; trust also in me.
In my Father's house are many
rooms; if it were not so, I would
have told you.
I am going there to prepare a
place for you.
And if I go and prepare a place
for you, I will come back and
take you to be with me that you
also may be where I am.
You know the way to the place
where I am going."
Thomas said to him, "Lord, we
don't know where you are going,
so how can we know the way?"
Jesus answered, "I am the way
and the truth and the life. No one
comes to the Father except
through me.
We will now sing our final
hymn Abide with me, please
stand"

SERVED COLD

They sang the hymn then the
curtains opened and the vicar
said a few more words as the
coffin made its way to cremation
to the Three Degrees song
"When will I see you again?"
Outside there were an enormous
amount of flowers, poor Lucy
met each mourner and thanked
them telling them the wake was
at the Spinning Jenny and they
were all welcome.
Back at the Spinning Jenny,
John made a bee line for Sheba,
in his sub conscious it was a
way of making Saron jealous.
The bar was full, Saron stood
with Donna and Wally while
John was stood with Sheba and
Shelley Etchings. With Shelley
not sure of the situation she
asked John had Saron and him
fallen out? "No nothing like that

SERVED COLD

Shelley" Sheba looked a bit bemused at the question. "Are you seeing Saron then John" she asked. "No, we are still friends though" "You are going to have to be for that baby" Sheba's face become more confused "baby"? "Yes, Saron is carrying John's baby, didn't you know?" "No I didn't" she said, clearly annoyed that John hadn't told her. At this point Sheba made an excuse and left John and Shelley and visited Carol Lestar and Jimmy.

"Sheba seemed upset John, did I drop you in it?" "No not really Shelley" "Well I certainly got the feeling I had" Just then, Saron, seeing Sheba had moved out, made her way over with Donna. "Hey John, Shelley, terrible thing about Ian" "Yes, it devastated the station to be

SERVED COLD

honest Saron" Saron didn't look
at John, basically ignoring him
and carried on speaking with
Shelley as if he wasn't there. It
became a bit embarrassing, so
John made his excuses and went
over to Janet and Dave Smarty
who were talking to Carl Milton.
"Can't believe Ian has gone
John, you did a really nice
eulogy" "Thanks Carl, he will
certainly be a loss to our team"
The day stayed on the same
theme as all funeral wakes do,
nice words said about the
person. John's thoughts were on
Sheba, Saron had really
aggravated him so he decided to
make a point. There were only
about eight or nine people left,
Shelley and Jack with Saron and
Sheba, Carl Milton talking to
Carol Lestar and Jimmy Lowcee

SERVED COLD

and a lady John didn't know at
the bar.

He wandered over to Sheba.
"Hey, can I have a word?"
Sheba followed him back to the
bar. "What do you want John
was that designed to make Saron
jealous?" Before John could
answer she set about the
situation of Saron being
pregnant. "Did you not think to
tell me? as if I wouldn't find
out" "Look I wasn't trying to
deceive you, you saw how Saron
is with me, to say we are frosty
is an understatement"

"So why the big fall out if you
are having a child together?"
"It's not been a fall out, I have
already been to one class with
her but the other night I called at
the Tow'd Man just to see when
we would be going again and

SERVED COLD

she was laughing and joking
with the guy who is
subcontracting at Pippa's Frozen
Foods, she basically ignored me
like tonight, anyway, enough is
enough, I'm not walking on egg
shells for her Sheba" John's
answer seemed to calm Sheba
down. "Yeah she was talking
about that Irish guy quite a lot,
she said you call him Paddy" "I
can never remember his name so
that always springs to mind"
Sheba laughed "I know you
better John Gammon" They
were engrossed in each other, by
the time John ordered another
drink Saron and Donna had left.
John's game-plan had worked,
he knew she still had feelings for
him so, as he had decided, he
was going to be the old John and
move on, another night spent

SERVED COLD

with Sheba somewhat convinced
him that the old John was back
in the game.

SERVED COLD

Chapter 8

The following morning at the station the team assembled in the incident room. "First of all, everybody, you did your colleague proud, we owe it to Ian Yap to crack this case and find his murderer as quickly as possible. Ok Wally, what do we have?" "The decomposed body threw up some problems for my team, like I said, he was tattooed like the others. This man had at some point had his arm broken in two places, he had a drug in him that would have paralysed him which was how our killer would have got him to the toilet block at Puddle Dale. We estimate he has been dead about three months, I can't tell you if his body was at the toilet block all the time or placed later, our

collective feeling is he was
maybe taken to the toilet block
three to four week ago and was
murdered somewhere else"
"Any DNA or fingerprints
Wally?" "No, sorry, we did well
to get what we did" "Ok thank
you, DS Bass come with me"
They closed the meeting and
Gammon and Bass were about
to leave when Magic said he had
a private call for DI Gammon.
"Ok put it through to my office,
here Kate, go and get in the car,
I won't be long" "Ok sir"
Gammon climbed the stairs to
his office. "This is DI Gammon,
how can I help?"
"Mr Gammon, just so you know,
I am not a monster, the body
you found, I'm sorry it
decomposed. There will be two,
maybe three more killings then

SERVED COLD

that will be my revenge done"
"Who is this, what revenge?"
"My mamma always said
"Revenge is a dish better served
cold" I have done as she
instructed. When my killing
spree is done I will then have
fulfilled my life and will no
longer have a need for it but you
will get an explanation for my
actions, I don't think you are a
bad man and I hope when you
get my letter you also think I am
not Mr Gammon" Gammon
tried to reason with the guy but
he just hung up. He wasn't on
long enough to even consider
trying to trace the call but he did
get the impression the man's
voice was an older man,
possibly in his sixties.
Gammon headed for the car, he
didn't mention to DS Bass about

SERVED COLD

the caller because if this guy
manages to do what he said he is
going to do and succeeds then he
will have a deflated squad. Just
at the moment his plan was to
build the team back up hence the
party he had organised. "Where
are we going sir?" "To the
Holocaust Museum near
Nottingham, somewhere in all
this lot there is a connection I'm
sure"
Gammon and Bass arrived and
the lady recognised Gammon.
"Oh, Inspector Gammon, I
mislaid your card and I have
found some more out for you"
"Oh that's great" "Look, I wrote
this all down the other night.
These are the tattoo numbers
you gave me, I already had some
names of the original tattoos
from the Concentration camp

SERVED COLD

which I gave you but have a full list now and some background for you. I put the tattoos against what you gave me Mr Gammon, "A11407 your victim, Ruth Weisner, the original tattoo was on Madgar Genk a Polish Jew who was interned in Auschwitz, B20081, Josef Guran, originally the tattoo was on Herschel Sparks also interned in Auschwitz, B20014, James Sinclair , the original tattoo was on Ezra Sully also a Polish Jew, B23318, Maurice Gates, the original tattoo was on Fritz Oglala, again a Polish Jew.

As you can see, these were all Polish Jews sent to the camp in-between Nineteen forty -one and two. I would guess that Herschel Sparks and Ezra Sully possibly knew each other with their

SERVED COLD

numbers so close. You will notice that the men are marked with a B and the one lady you gave me with an A, this was how the Nazi's set up their filing system. I did find out that Madgar Genk and Josef Guran were listed on the same train but I don't know if that has any significance"

"If they were on the same train where might they have met?"

"Well they were certainly from the same ghetto Mr Gammon"

"Ok, sadly I have another name I wondered if you could help me with. We had another victim, Bernard Dyan, he was tattooed with this number B33101. I'm afraid the body was badly decomposed but by luck the tattoo was just visible"

"Just a moment Mr Gammon, oh I am so sorry, would you both

SERVED COLD

like a coffee?" "That's very kind of you" "I'm sorry, it's just been so busy of late, that was very rude of me" "Hey, no worries, thank you" "What a nice lady sir" "Yes, very helpful" "Would you mind if I took a look around?" "No go-ahead Kate, great work these people do, we must never forget what these poor people went through" "And still are sir" "Yes you are correct Kate" Gammon started drinking his coffee trying in his mind to figure out why these tattoo's, it seems like the killer is somehow trying to tell us something.

Twenty minutes passed when the lady came back with more information. "Ok Mr Gammon, you have been lucky, Bernard Dyan's tattoo was originally on a German Jew called Frankel

SERVED COLD

Hosentstie" "Thank you" "Just a moment, I have more, we know quite a bit about Frankel Mr Gammon, he was a Nazi sympathiser and somehow achieved the status of an SS officer until Nineteen forty three when, one night, he was drunk in a bar in Dresden and he blurted out that he was a German Jew. Within minutes he was taken away and found himself in Auschwitz. Once word got around he was severely beaten many times. Eventually they decided to make him a Kapo" "A Kapo?" "Well, they used the Jewish inmates to do their dirty work by making them Kappa's" "What do you mean by dirty work?" "They would herd the people to the gas chambers, they were also known as prison functionaries. They were generally recruited from the violent criminals in the camp so it was a fair bet that Frankel Hosentstie was a criminal although I don't know that for a fact Mr Gammon. These men were hated by the Jews, they were very violent towards the prisoners and it was mainly ignored by the German officers, that's the best I have Mr Gammon" "Thank you Mary, you have been a fantastic help" Gammon placed a twenty- pound note in the museum charity box. "Thank you, if you need any more help please call me" "I will Mary, thank you" DS Bass had missed most of the conversation and her eyes looked as if she had been crying. When they got to the car Gammon asked if she was ok.

SERVED COLD

"Sorry sir, yes, I just can't believe what they did to those poor people, how can anybody be so inhuman" "I don't know Kate, it's beyond me"

Gammon drove them back and checked with Magic if all was ok, he said it seemed quiet. Then Gammon realised he hadn't asked Magic to the party tomorrow night so took the opportunity, "Thank you sir, am I ok to bring my girlfriend?" "Of course, not a problem"

John decided to write down what Mary had told him just to see if he could get some connection, it was now almost 6.0ppm and he referenced the names again and again. The only thing standing out was one was a German Jew, the rest were Polish Jews, then it hit him, Josef Guran's tattoo had

SERVED COLD

been on somebody called Hershel Sparks, DS Bass had found out that Guran's mother's maiden name was Sparks. He quickly phoned Abigail but there was no answer then he realised it was meeting night for the Jewish Community in Ackbourne Town Hall. Gammon grabbed his coat and raced downstairs. "See you tomorrow night Magic, ask Di Trimble if she can get one of the beat lads to do her shift, she is welcome to come" "Will do sir" John raced to Ackbourne feeling he was onto something, he had a connection perhaps. He parked in the cobbled market square and raced to the Town Hall. He had just timed it right, they were just about to go in so he waited whilst acknowledging one or two that Abigail had introduced him too.

SERVED COLD

By 7.30pm they were ready to close the door but there was no sign of Abigail, then his phone rang. "Sir, just taken a call from a gentleman who was out walking his dog and he has found a body" "Where Magic?" "Castleting sir" "Have you informed Wally?" "Yes and I managed to get hold DS Bass and DI Milton, they are on their way" "Ok I'll set off now Magic"

John left Ackbourne frustrated he hadn't seen Abigail but now he had another murder on his hands, when will this ever stop he thought as he drove to Castleting. In his mind he knew they had only one suspect and at best that was flimsy. If this was the killer that meant he would kill one more time if he was true to his

SERVED COLD

word so time was running out and John knew it.

He arrived at the murder scene, Wally's white tent was blowing in the wind and he could see DS Bass and DI Milton talking to a guy. "Good evening, DI Gammon, Bixton Police and you are?" "This is Mick Sutton sir, he was out walking Panda" "Panda?" "Sorry sir, his Newfoundland dog" "Where is it now Mr Sutton?" "I called my wife. we only live over there, I told her what had happened and that I had to stay to be questioned by the police" "Ok Mr Sutton, is this your regular walk with your dog?" Gammon couldn't call the dog Panda, it seemed a silly name to him. "I get home from work usually about 5.15pm then have my dinner and usually me and the wife walk the dog, luckily tonight she was making a dress for our daughter's school play, I'm so glad she didn't see what Panda found Mr Gammon" "Ok Mr Sutton, if we have any more questions we will be in touch. Before you go, you didn't see anybody lurking about did you?" "There were three kids playing at the bottom of the hill but up here no" "Ok, thank you, DI Milton will take your address. DS Bass can you go over to the Holocaust Museum tomorrow morning and see if Mary has got anything on this tattoo once Wally gives it me?" "No problem sir" "I would go myself but with the party I have a few things to do" "Yes that's fine sir" "Right, let me speak with Wally" Gammon took the usual spat of annoyance from

SERVED COLD

Wally for putting his head in the tent and he came out.

"Anything yet Wally?" "Not really mate, I would say early twenties, tattooed like the others" "What's the number?" "B33311" "Ok Wally, well if you can get me the information for Monday please. Are you and the wife coming tomorrow night?" "What, me miss a free bar? you bet we are John" "Ok mate, look forward to seeing you"

"Ok Carl, wrap it up here, DS Bass, give me a call if we have any luck with Mary at the Holocaust Museum" "Ok, will do sir" John left and decided to call at the Spinning Jenny just to make sure about the party.

The pub was surprisingly quiet for a Friday night, just Wez behind the bar, a party of four

SERVED COLD

who looked like walkers and Jimmy Lowcee. "What are you having John?" "I'll have a Pedigree please Jimmy, no Carol tonight?" "No, her mum's been a bit off it so she wanted to say in with her" "So you got a free pass then Jimmy?" "Yeah something like that. What time does the party start tomorrow?" "I think 7.30pm don't you Wez?" "Yes mate that's fine, Tony Baloney usually starts setting up about 6.00pm anyway mate"

"Are there many coming John?" "I'm guessing at least sixty Jimmy" "Should be a good do then" "Hope so, the lads have been under a lot of pressure at work so it will give them a chance to let off steam"

John stuck it until 10.00pm then headed home, on the way he

SERVED COLD

called Abigail Harrop. "Hi Abigail, listen I am throwing a party Saturday night at the Spinning Jenny and you have been such a help, I wondered if you would like to come? By all means bring a friend" "Oh Mr Gammon that's very kind of you, I would love to come" "No more Mr Gammon, its John or DI Gammon on duty" "Ok, thanks John, see you Saturday night, any specific time?" "It will start at 7.30pm so as early as you wish, thanks again for your help Abigail, it's been invaluable" John arrived home to find DC had been bored, she had clawed the arm of the settee. "You are naughty DC" John said in a firm tone. It didn't matter to DC, she just purred and wrapped herself around John's legs. John quickly

made himself a tuna mayo
sandwich, ate it and headed for
bed.

The following morning John had
overlay, it was almost 10.30am, it
was something he never did but
maybe the pressure was telling on
him as well. Just before lunch DS
Bass called." Hi sir" "Hello Kate,
how did you get on?" "Quite
good sir, the tattoo, B33311 was
originally on a polish Jew, Remo
Gunter. By the accounts
smuggled out of Auschwitz when
they were liberated Remo Gunter
had saved many Jews by telling
the SS Officers that they were
accountants or seamstresses,
anything that the SS needed, he
was finally found out when a girl
named Heidi, sorry they didn't
have a surname, had told Remo
she could read and write so he

SERVED COLD

said she would be a good bookkeeper but sadly she couldn't so they sent her to the gas chamber with poor Remo Gunter behind her as a warning. Luckily, the others that he had saved would most possibly have been gassed but the liberators arrived, the SS, a lot of them ran for their lives. So now we have to try and figure out the name of the victim, hopefully Wally will have that on Monday and maybe, just maybe, we can start getting some kind of picture on what the connection is"

"Good work Kate, see you tonight" "Looking forward to it sir" John had everything set up and headed at 7.00pm to the Spinning Jenny, he was almost there when his phone rang, it was Saron. "John, I think you are

SERVED COLD

being very petty about my Irish friend and to not invite me and Donna to the party is just ridiculous" "I did invite Donna" "Oh, so it is just me in the Peak District that doesn't warrant an invite"

"Saron, I really don't want to argue, I have seen you twice now and each time you made me feel like I was mud under your boots so if anyone is being petty it's you" and he cut the call. For John to do that he knew he had turned the corner, he had been married to Lindsay and she tried to control him and there was no way that was happening again he thought. John arrived at The Spinning Jenny and Lindsay's sister Chocolate, as they called her, had decorated the pub to add even more atmosphere. John

SERVED COLD

thanked her and she asked if he was going to the opening night the following Thursday for the bistro in Swinster called Dog House, "You must come" said the guy stood with Chocolate. "Sorry, John Gammon, this is my dad Sid and the dog is called Nellie, you can stroke her, she won't bite all your arm off" and he laughed. "Take her in the back Dad it's going to be busy" "Come on Nellie, they won't let you stay old girl" Sid dragged her down the corridor much to the annoyance of Nellie.

By 8.30pm it was packed, John was pleased all the team had come with their respective partners, they were dancing and laughing. John hadn't seen that in the team for a long while. Sheba arrived with Jack and Shelley,

SERVED COLD

they shared a taxi. Sheba looked
fabulous John thought, she had
on a white dress with large black
flower prints, she had her
beautiful black hair sort of half up
and half down, she certainly
stood out. "Come on John, we are
dancing to this" an early Bon Jovi
song. John wasn't much of a
heavy rock fan but he knew
Sheba liked it so went to dance.
They were on the dance floor for
three records so John was glad
when Lindsay announced the
buffet was ready in the bottom
room.

It was almost 11.00pm when
Abigail arrived, she said she had
fallen asleep. "No problem, there
is plenty of food left, enjoy
yourself" and John went off to
find Sheba. "So Miss Gorgeous,
we are going to have a bit of chat

SERVED COLD

time" "Blimey, is this really John Gammon?

I see there is no Saron?" "No, we have argued because I didn't invite her" "Blimey you really are trying to cut tie's" she said draping her arms around his neck and, standing on her tip toes she placed a kiss on his lips.

The night was a resounding success, he could tell his team were in a good place.

It was almost 1.35am when Wez said he would drop John off at home as he hadn't had a drink with working, Sheba had gone back with Jack and Shelley, she had quite a few lambs to sort.

The following morning John felt good, he had held the party and he had also decided his fate with Saron. He would be part of the baby's life and support it of

SERVED COLD

course but how Saron was now
he couldn't see a way forward for
those two so he would get on
with his life.

He cooked a bacon sandwich and
watched the Andrew Marr show
before setting off for a walk. He
had to pick his car up and pay
Wez so the plan was he would do
a six hour walk and end up at the
Spinning Jenny.

John set off with a few layers on
as it was quite a cold morning, he
decided to go past Sheba's fields
to see if he could see her.

It was 10.20am when he arrived
at the fields next to Sheba's
cottage and she was actually
attending to a lamb. "Hey John,
thanks for last night I really
enjoyed it" John smiled. "What's
with the smile?" "Nothing, just
thinking that last night you were

SERVED COLD

all dressed up and today you have an old wax jacket and some wellies on yet you still look gorgeous" "Give over Gammon, where are you headed for?" "Doing a six hour walk then land at the Spinning Jenny to get my car" "Oh, did you get a taxi last night?" "No Wez took me home" "That was good of him John" "Yes they are a really great couple"

"Do you want a drink before you set off up the fields?" "No, I'm ok Sheba, I'm not sure about this weather, it looks like it might rain" "If you want I will be done in two hours, I could run you for your car" "Thanks for the offer but I need to sweat some of that alcohol out of my system"

"Ok, give me a call in the week John" "Will do" and he kissed

her and headed up the steep climb
for Pommie and Waterdale, he
could have cut the steep climb
out but wanted the exercise. He
eventually stood on the peak of
Waterdale looking down on the
picturesque village.

He stood for possibly twenty
minutes speaking with different
walkers as they passed by before
heading towards Cuckoo Dale. It
was quite windy on the top as he
walked towards Cuckoo Dale.
Cuckoo Dale over the years had
been scarred by lead mining and
spa mining but in a funny way it
gave the place character. John
had a few minutes before
carrying on towards the beautiful
Dumpling Dale which was
always busy at this time of a
weekend so, as beautiful as it was
John headed for Monkdale and

SERVED COLD

The Sloppy Quiche Café. He was
feeling a bit hungry and it was
now almost 1.20pm so he stopped
to see Karen and Jimmy Jigley, it
was always a busy café because
the food was so good. "Hey John,
how lovely to see you, I was only
saying to Jimmy last night that
we hadn't seen you in ages" "Just
had so much on with work Karen,
how's Jimmy?" "Off today with
Man flu !! my mums cooking and
helping out. So, are you stopping
for something to eat John or is
this just a passing visit?" "No I'll
have a table and I know what I
want" Karen interrupted him. "A
strong black coffee?" "You got it
Karen and I'll have one of your
cheese and broccoli quiches with
baby new potatoes and salad
please" "Sit over there, table
three John by the window and I

SERVED COLD

will have it straight up" "Thanks
Karen"

True to her word the food took
five minutes and the quiche was
fabulous, in fact the whole meal
was. John finished his meal and
paid Karen, he was just leaving
when he bumped into Roger
Glazeback coming in. "Hey
Roger, how are you? I didn't
know you were a walker, would
have thought you got enough
exercise with the farm" "We
parked the car at Up the Steps
Maggie's and wandered on so no
real exercise mate" "Have you
had a quiche?" "Yes mate, cheese
and broccoli, fabulous" "Tell you
what John, Karen and Jimmy
certainly made a go of this place"
"Yeah good food, great service,
great views and nice people,
guaranteed success Roger"

SERVED COLD

"Reckon you are right" "Well look mate, best get on my way" "Go steady John, you aren't as young as you were" and Roger laughed.

John headed for Swinster, it was almost 3.50pm and the bar was quiet, Wez had taken his boy to football so Carol Lestar was doing the bar. "Hey John, great night last night, me and Jimmy really enjoyed it" "Thanks Carol, did Wez leave me a bill?" "Let me have a look, there is an envelope with John Gammon written on it" She handed it John and he opened it, it just said two hundred and ninety-seven pounds plus eighty-five pound for Tony Maloney (Disco). "Did it hurt John?" "No, actually it's cheaper than I expected" Just then the bar door flung open and five dogs,

SERVED COLD

four Jack Russel's and one springer spaniel came crashing in with a small petite lady. "Has he been good Louise?" "Your King Power is a star Carol" "Oh, John, this is my friend Louise Winalot" "Great name Louise seeing that you clearly love dogs, get everyone a drink Carol and add it to this bill. So Louise, what do you do for a living?" "Call me Lou, I prefer that" "Ok Lou" "I have a veterinary practice in Winksworth" "Oh right, I have a cat so will remember that, do you have a card?" Lou handed John her business card.

"That's great, if DC gets sick I know where to come. Have you walked far?" Almost twenty miles then I always call and have a drink with Carol but usually she is this side of the bar"

SERVED COLD

John chatted until 7.00pm, he called at Dilley Dale and got a Chinese take-away then headed home. DC was pleased as always to see him. He decided on an early night, his thought was tomorrow could be a big day with the case.

SERVED COLD

Chapter 9

The following morning John headed for Bixton arriving just as everyone was heading for the incident room. "Ok everybody, Wally is going to run through what he has found with the body and DS Bass will fill you all in on the tattoo and what she found out, Ok Wally, over to you"

Wally stood up, "Well, the body was tattooed like the others, B33311, he was a male aged between thirty-two and thirty-five, he was drugged, tattooed then murdered and not where you found him, he was taken there for some reason. His dental records show him to be one Henrik James of number 3 Station Cottages, Rowksly" "Ok Wally, DS Bass?" Kate stood up. "Ok, Saturday morning I revisited The

SERVED COLD

Holocaust Museum to see if the tattoo number on the latest victim meant anything to anyone, it was very interesting, the tattoo number B33311 found on our victim Henrik James was originally on a Polish Jew called Remo Gunter. Now this is where it seems confusing, up until now my thinking, like I'm sure all yours, would have been that there is some connection with the victims and the original owners of the tattoo's. Remo Gunter tried and did succeed in saving many Jews from the gas chambers, he was eventually found out and was also sent to the gas chamber, my question is, why would the killer kill someone who was basically a hero? Yes, DI Smarty" "I think our killer just doesn't like Jews and I think DS Yap was hot on the trail and was killed because he knew too much. I think we should put a permanent trace on Marty Baynes, I do believe he will lead us eventually to the killer if it's not him its somebody in his organisation"

"Good point DI Smarty, seeing that it's your idea if you do the day shift and DI Lee, you do the night shift for two weeks and let's see what we get from it" Gammon wasn't convinced with DI Smarty's appraisal but didn't want his officer thinking there was only one view point and that being his.

Gammon dismissed the meeting and headed for his office feeling they were still no further forward. The Remo Gunter killing didn't make sense like the others, come

SERVED COLD

to think about it, why was Myra killed and DS Yap?

The view to Losehill was dramatic today, it was very windy out. Gammon stood gazing hoping for inspiration, nothing was forth coming so he sat down to work on his reports which had started to pile up again. It was almost 6.40pm when John realised the time, his desk was now almost clear so he called it a night. Before he left he rang Kev and arranged to meet him for one at the Spinning Jenny, Kev said Doreen would drop him off on her way to Badminton at Pritwich Village Hall.

John arrived and Kev was on his second bottle. "Where have you been lad?" "Sorry Kev, just finished off at work" "Doreen was going as you rang so I was

SERVED COLD

early" "You can tell it pained him John, I mean, dropped off early at a pub!" "I know Wez, he's a wily old lad aren't you Kev?" Kev just gave him that knowing smile. "So how are you and Saron now?" "It's about done Kev" John explained what happened and that he was a free agent and was seeing Sheba a bit. "Bloody hell lad, you don't half have some good- looking women" "Charisma Kev" "Bloody luck I would say" and Kev laughed. Here lads try these. "What are they Wez?" "It's mashed potato, white cabbage with cheddar cheese rolled in breadcrumbs then deep fat fried" Kev's eyes lit up, "Don't tell our Doreen, she has had me on bloody salads all last week, blimey Wez, these are fabulous, are they one of your

SERVED COLD

creations?" "No, Lindsay was looking through an old Irish cook book mainly for some vegetarian dishes and she came across these so she said to hand some out to the locals to see what they think Kev" "Well I think they are brilliant tell Lindsay" "Will do mate"

By 9.00 pm John and Kev had hit the brandy bottle with Wez having the odd one with them. At 9.40pm the girls arrived from badminton, Sheba, Doreen, Shelley, Tracey Rogers and Donna Fringe which John was quite shocked at. "What are you drinking girls?" "I'm ok John, just come to get Kev, we have a salad with our names on them don't we love?" Kev smiled at John and Wez knowing he'd had his fill of the cabbage things.

SERVED COLD

The girls all ordered and Donna wandered over to John. "Come on then lover boy, what have you said to Saron?" "Why what has she said?" "She has been in a foul mood since the other night and I actually caught her crying in the kitchen on Saturday night" "Oh she was annoyed because I didn't invite her to the party on Saturday night" "Why didn't you John? You know she is deeply in love with you" Well she has a funny way of showing it Donna, just when I think we are close to getting back together she pulls up the drawbridge and I'm all deflated so I decided to get on with my life and see who I want to see" "Oh John, we have been friends a long time, don't throw your relationship with Saron away, you have to remember she

SERVED COLD

felt let down big style on her wedding day, now she is pregnant so that will be playing on her mind" "I don't know Donna, it's up to her, I have done all the running since our wedding day and probably rightly so but no more, if she wants a relationship she needs to come to me now" Sheba came over, "You two look serious" "No just talking about when we worked together, best get back and have a chat with Shelley and leave you two to it" John's head was mashed, now what he thought? The last thing he wanted to do was hurt Sheba, she was a stunning girl and he was really enjoying her company, he didn't feel under any pressure with her.

"Are you coming back to mine John?" "Can't refuse that Sheba"

SERVED COLD

"Ok then, I can bring you for your car in the morning" "Sounds good to me" It was soon 11.00pm and the pub was virtually empty except for Sheba and John so they called it a night. Sheba said to make them both a drink then bring them up while she showered. John took the coffees up to the bedroom and she came out of the bathroom wrapped in a fluffy white bath sheet her jet-black hair dripping then she dropped the towel to display her perfectly formed body. John began kissing her neck then worked his way down, Sheba was writhing in ecstasy as they fell on her king-sized bed.

The foreplay lasted for almost an hour before they finally succumbed to their desires leaving them bot breathless at the

SERVED COLD

end. John knew Sheba was in some way trying to prove to John that Saron was no match for her. They lay with Sheba's head on his chest. "So, what were you and Donna really talking about John?" John didn't want a relationship built on lies so he decided to be honest and told her everything they had discussed. "Look John, I want you to be honest with me, I'm not the type of girl that is constantly wanting attention but if this keeps happening I don't want to be used either, does that sound fair to you?" "Sheba that's more than fair" and he kissed her passionately.

The following morning she had made him a bacon sandwich but he took it with him, he wanted to get into work, he was sure that

SERVED COLD

the Assistant Chief Constable
would be calling soon as the local
radio station was running a phone
in at 10.00 am about the murders
and the performance of Bixton
Police and they rarely went well.
Gammon was mindful that the
killer had said he would strike
again and all would be revealed,
he would sooner catch him than
be told it wouldn't look good for
him or Bixton Station.

John sat with a pair of
headphones on in his office
listening to Peak-side Radio
Station. "Good morning my
lovely audience, this is Andy
Strikes your DJ right through
until 1.00pm. The first hour is
dedicated to the serial killer
stalking the Jewish Community. I
want your views, are the Police
doing enough? Are they beat with

SERVED COLD

this one? Should DI Gammon, who is heading up the case, be removed, is he inept do you think? If you are listening DI Gammon and want to say your piece it's a free world, phone in, we would love to hear from you. Right let's take the first call and it's from Agnes Bosch from Rowksly, good morning Agnes thanks for contacting us, what have you got to say?" "I think your phone in is wrong, Bixton Police and in particular DI John Gammon are working hard to solve this case and where would we be without them?" "Thank you Agnus, clearly a John Gammon fan, you are not his aunty are you?" and he laughed. "Next caller on the line please" "Hi, I'm Derek from Dilley Dale, well if the previous caller thinks the police are working hard can somebody tell me why they were all getting drunk at a party I believe was thrown by DI Gammon only a few days after he had cremated one of his fellow officers?" "Were you there Derek?" "At the pub?" "Yes, at the pub where the party was taking place?"

"I was there with my wife until about 10.00pm and if that's our police that is going to protect the Jewish community then we have a problem" "Ok thanks Derek, Sandra is on line three, she is from Ackbourne, what would you like to say Sandra?" "I work at the biscuit factory where Ruth Weisner worked before she was murdered and she was an oddball" "Sorry Sandra, can't have you speaking ill of the dead,

SERVED COLD

let's move swiftly on. Paul from Micklock" "Hi, my point is they have cut resources and Bixton was part of the cuts but we expect our police force to carry on as if nothing has happened, I blame the Government for this mess. If they shut Bixton Station like they are threatening to then the people in the High Peak would not have a police station for thirty- five miles. You can do a robbery and be away in thirty -five minutes" "Good point Paul, so far we are getting more callers on the side of the police than the other way around, our next caller, yes my friend, what's your name?" "I don't want to give my name but to tell you that there will only be one more killing then it will be over" "I'm sorry, are you saying you are the killer or you know the killer?" The man hung up, Gammon knew the voice and he knew it was the killer. John had heard enough, he knew that time was running out for somebody but there was nothing he could do. He had spoken with DI Smarty and DI Lee, both said they had seen nothing untoward with Marty Baynes, besides John thought, when he had spoken with the killer it wasn't Baynes' voice.

The frustration Gammon was feeling was beyond words, what the hell was the connection other than they were Jewish and had been tattooed with the same tattoos as some in mates from Auschwitz?

SERVED COLD

Chapter 10

Almost a month had passed, Saron hadn't contacted John and he hadn't been to any more anti-natal classes, he had seen Sheba a few times and taken Tracey Rogers out a couple of times and was generally just being a single guy. It was 4.00pm when John took a call from Mary at the Holocaust Museum. "Mr Gammon?" "Good afternoon Mary, how can I help you?" "I have found the connection!" "I'm sorry, please explain" "The tattoos of the men I gave you?" "Yes, what about them?" "All these men were Kapo's except for Remo Gunter, he had tried to save many of the Jewish people but was eventually found out and was gassed"

SERVED COLD

"Mary, excuse my ignorance
what exactly did a Kapo do?"
"He did the dirty work for the SS
and he would have been a Jew as
well. They really were horrible to
the prisoners and that is what was
expected by the SS officers. They
were cruel men, there are reports
of them seeing their wives and
young children standing in line
for a shower, as they thought,
then being gassed and these men
were more interested in surviving
themselves than looking after
their wives and children. They
were despised after the war and
were hunted down, many were
killed but many escaped to the
UK, America and South America.
Because all the paperwork was
lost, they were untraceable"
"Mary I can't thank you enough"

SERVED COLD

"Not a problem Mr Gammon, I am always willing to help" Gammon suddenly realised because Hendrik James lived on his own he should go over to meet the landlord who owned the property to let him know Mr James had passed away. Gammon ran to his car and raced over to Rowksly to Hendrik James cottage, the landlord was there and some guys with a van, they were about to do a house clearance. "I'm very sorry I can't let you do this until we have done a sweep on the property" "I have just paid for these guys to clear the place" "Sorry but there may be evidence in the house that could lead to this man's killer" The landlord stood shaking his head. Gammon left him to it and went inside, he called the station

SERVED COLD

and told DS Bass and DI Milton to come over and help him search. They spent almost four hours searching through everything then were just about to give up when DS Bass screamed with delight. "Sir, look" in an inside pocket of a sports jacket was a letter it read.

"Dear Hendrik,

As you know our ancestors did good things in the name of our beloved leader, most of the Jews were stupid and deserved their fate.

You are safe Hendrik, do not worry, keep your nerve for our day will arrive and we must be ready"

The letter wasn't signed Gammon popped it into a forensic bag and set off back to see Wally telling

SERVED COLD

the other two to keep
looking. He raced back to
the station just as Wally
was about to leave for the
day, Gammon gave him the
letter and he said he would
stay and come in early the
next day so that he would
have results for the 9.00am
meeting.

John decided there was nothing
more he could do so decided on
an early night by the fire, the
nights were drawing in now. He
had just settled down with one of
Phyllis Swan's home-made
lasagnes and a large Jameson
when his phone rang, it was DI
Milton, "John we have another
victim, a man, he is pretty cut up
to the point of hardly being
recognisable, his private parts
have been removed and pushed in

his mouth, this is a bad John"
"Where are you Carl?" "I'm at
Trissington, the man was found
by the head gardener for
Trissington Hall, he has a vague
description of a man he thought
was dumping rubbish, he went to
investigate and found the body"
"Carl I'm on my way, keep the
man there, has Wally been
informed?" "He is setting his tent
up now" "Good, ok mate, see you
in about twenty minutes"
John knew that was the last one
that the case was over and he
fully expected somebody to
contact him. He arrived at
Trissington, the village was so
picturesque with all the lights on
and the little houses all painted
the same colour with neat small
gardens where the estate workers
lived.

SERVED COLD

Gammon could see Carl with two beat lads and another guy with a hat like Sherlock Holmes wore in the books, he assumed that was the head gardener. "Good evening" Gammon flashed his warrant card, "So you are the gentleman that found the body?" "Correct" "What's your name?" "Eddie Lipton, I'm head gardener at Trissington Hall, you are the guy that jilted Saron at the alter aren't you?" Gammon felt a bit embarrassed, "I'm not here to discuss my private life Mr Lipton. So what time did you find the body?" "He rang the call in at 7.35pm sir" "How did you come across the body?" I was locking up the sheds where we keep the ride on mowers etc and I saw somebody down by the Olde Sweetshop and I assumed he was

fly tipping so I shouted at him.
He dropped the load he had on
his back and ran that way" Lipton
pointed beyond the shop. "So he
went that way, did he have a
vehicle?" "Yes but it was too
dark to see what make it was, I
think it was dark green but I can't
be sure on that"
Gammon got on his phone.
"Magic, bit of a long shot but tell
the traffic lads to look for a dark
green van" and he explained what
had happened. "Ok sir, will do"
"Ok Mr Lipton, here is my card,
if you can recall anything else
please let me know even if you
think it's insignificant, thanks for
your help and I'm sorry for your
shock" "No worries" and he
wandered back to the Hall.
Gammon stuck his head round
the tent and got the obligatory

SERVED COLD

telling off from Wally for contaminating the crime scene. "What you got Wally?" This was quite a frenzied attack on a man in his late seventies, early eighties" "Was he tattooed?" "Yes he was but not on his chest, this was under his arm" "How weird, what is the number Wally?" "That's just it John, it's under his left arm and it's just a capital A and a capital B in black ink and that's it, I nearly missed it or assumed it was a different killer" "Ok Wally, if you can have something for the morning that would be great" "Will do my best John" "Ok Carl, call it a night, leave the beat lads watching the scene and let's hope Wally comes up with something" "Ok, see you at the meeting tomorrow" John went straight

SERVED COLD

back to his lasagne and
Jameson's, thankfully DC hadn't
spotted it with him rushing out.

SERVED COLD

Chapter 11

Almost a month had gone by and the killings appeared to have stopped, John hadn't been contacted and the team still had nobody in the frame for DS Yap's murder, Myra Sinclair or the seven tattooed murders, one of which was only tattooed with AB under the armpit of the left arm. Gammon called Mary at the Holocaust Museum.

"Hi Mary, really sorry to bother you again but we have had another murder but this time the tattoo was under the left arm and it simply said AB in black ink" Mary went quiet for a minute. "Mr Gammon that would have been an SS officer and quite likely, if he was in the death camps, an SD officer" "What does that mean?" "They were the

most evil and cruel people chosen
for the task of the extermination
of our people, AB was for his
blood group. Most, not all of the
Waffen SS had these tattoo's, the
thinking was if they were injured
in the field and needed blood it
was taken from a fellow officer
with the same blood type"

"Wow this is really eye opening,
thank you Mary, I really
appreciate your help"

Gammon then decided to call
Abigail to see if there were any
further members not attending the
Friday night meetings. "Yes Mr
Gammon, we haven't seen Robin
for over a month and nobody
knew where he lived so we
assumed he must have passed
away, he was in his early
seventies" "So what was Robins
surname?" "Lensky, his name

SERVED COLD

was Robin Lensky" "Was he a Jew?" "Well, funny you should say that, I had a conversation a couple of weeks back with one of the elders and we both said he didn't look Jewish, you know we tend to have large noses but he had always said he was a German Jew, that his father was in Auschwitz and when they were liberated by the Russians he said he met his wife and quite quickly Robin was born then they were settled in England. Sadly, his father died in nineteen fifty-two and his mum brought him up but she died in nineteen sixty-three, by now he was working in a bank in Micklock until he retired in two thousand and ten"

"Would the bank know where he lived?" "I guess so Mr Gammon" "Ok, thanks Abigail" "No thank you for trying to find this evil person that is terrorising our community"

Gammon rang of then started ringing the banks in Micklock, problem was most had shut down since 2010. Eventually he got through to the RBS Bank and the manager remembered working with Robin Lensky at the Midland bank which is now a bar but he gave Gammon Midland banks' office HR division number.

Gammon eventually got through to Alison Sparming who gave him the last known address of Robin Lensky that they had when he retired, The View, Stinton Dale, Stinton. Gammon called DS Bass and said they were going over to see if this was the home of Robin Lensky.

SERVED COLD

Stinton was a small former quarry village with a pub, a post office about eighty houses and a small camp site. Gammon and Bass found The View, it was a semi-detached bungalow so Gammon knocked on the next-door neighbour's door to check. "Excuse me, I'm very sorry to bother you, I am DI Gammon and this is my colleague DS Bass and I wondered if the house next door is the home of a gentleman called Robin Lensky?" "Yes that's Robin's place but I think he has gone home for a month, he quite often does that since he retired." "Was he married?" "No, Robin is a shy man, he would colour up if I spoke to him, a good neighbour though. I know he used to go to that Jewish Community place at Ackbourne, he once told me his

poor father had been in
Auschwitz during the war but
that's about all I know"

"Well I'd best inform you that we
are investigating the death of Mr
Lensky"

"What!! Oh dear, how sad, I was
expecting him to be back anytime
soon" "Well just so you know,
unless you have a key for his
place we are going to have to
break in" "Robin always kept a
key under his milk bottle holder
by the back door in case of a
problem when he used to go
home so I could go in and check
on things. I never did to be
honest, I don't like entering
somebodies' home, it's their
space isn't it Mr Gammon?" "I
guess so Mrs?" "Mrs Harriet
Long" "Thank you Harriet"
Gammon and Bass walked down

SERVED COLD

the garden path and headed to
The View.

Sure enough the key was under
the milk bottle stand so they
entered through the kitchen. The
kitchen was very old fashioned
and smelt a bit damp, the next
room was the dining room with a
table and four chairs which
looked like they had never been
used. In one corner was a small
coffee table with a framed
certificate which read "FOR
ROBIN LENSKY FOR
FOURTY YEARS DEDICATED
SERVICE TO THE MICKLOCK
BRANCH"

They headed for the Living room
which was quite sparse with a
small maybe sixteen inch
television in one corner and a
radio in the other corner, hung on
the wall were photographs of

SERVED COLD

mountains that Gammon assumed
Mr Lensky had taken from his
holidays over the years, "Ok
Kate, let's look in the bedrooms"
In the first bedroom which was
used, nothing seemed out of place
but in the second bedroom there
was a filing cabinet and a desk
with what looked like a journal.
It appeared that Robin Lensky
was writing about his family. "It
started in June 1962. My mother
called me to her house, she said
she had something to share with
me, I arrived eager to know what
was going on. When I arrived,
mother had been crying, I asked
her what the problem was and she
passed me a letter that my father
had written just before he died. It
was like mum knew she hadn't
got long and I eventually lost my
sweet mother in nineteen sixty-

SERVED COLD

three. This is the content of the letter addressed to mum.

"My Dearest Ruth,

What I am about to tell you will undoubtedly shock you to the core. My real name is Paul Seeler, I was born in Berlin, my father fought in the first World War and preached hatred against the Jews, he believed we lost the war because of them, so it was not surprising that I was indoctrinated and also hated the Jews. When I was a young man, Hitler started to come to power, we idolised him because he was saying what the German people were thinking. I joined Hitler's party and became somewhat of a rising star in the Waffen SS, I was eventually assigned to Auschwitz and was an SD, I suppose you know that is the

SERVED COLD

worst kind. We were trained to be evil and because of my upbringing it was the perfect job. I will not go into all the things I did but I honestly do not regret anything. When the Russians came I had worked out that if I dressed like a Jew I might get out, which I did. My life changed when I met you dear Ruth, you were Jewish but I fell in love. You don't know how many sleepless nights I had, how could I tell this beautiful caring lady that I had been an animal to her race and possibly even killed her relatives.?

I decided that I would write this letter and leave it for you to read when I die, if you go before me then I would leave it for Robin. This is the only way I can redeem

SERVED COLD

myself. I hope you both understand.

Until we meet again my love"

Paul

Xxxxxx

"Wow sir, that is some heavy stuff. When you read it and he says he had no regrets but is looking for redemption, this guy was a nut case. Can you imagine their Son Robin carrying this guilt with him all these years and being brought up as a Jew as well!" "Let's get back Kate, take this with us, get all the team together" It was almost 3.00pm when they assembled. "Ok listen up everybody, our last victim a month ago was a guy called Robin Lensky, he worked in a bank in Micklock until he retired, he was brought up as a Jew but we have discovered his father

SERVED COLD

was a Waffen SS and SD officer
in Auschwitz. All the tattoos
were people who I think had a
connection to the people with the
original tattoos from Auschwitz,
now we have this one which was
a far more frenzied attack. So it's
almost positive our killer is a
relation I guess of somebody
abused by these ancestors of our
victims. I would have to guess
that DS Yap had fallen on all this
by chance and was trying to piece
this together but our killer, for
some strange reason, needed to
murder all the people he did
having stated the last one would
be his last killing and its since
gone quiet. I believe that Myra
was killed because of the picture
she had, so we have a reason
now, we need to find the killer. I
want door to door, I want every

SERVED COLD

avenue explored, the Jewish
Survivors club, I want every
member investigated with
urgency team" Gammon was
beginning to think he was getting
closer, it was almost 7.00pm
when he left work fully intending
to get a take away from the
Spinning Jenny. John was
travelling through Swinster when
his phone rang, it was Donna
Fringe. "John, Saron has been in
a car accident on Micklock Moor,
you need to get over to Derby
Royal, it isn't good" John's heart
was racing as he headed to the
hospital. He stopped at the front
desk and asked for the ward,
"Just a moment sir, are you a
relative? her mother is here
already" John knew they might
not tell him anything so he said
he was her fiancé. "Well she is in

the operating theatre at the minute but if you wish to go to Smedley ward her mother is there and hopefully that's where they will take her, that is one of the high dependency wards. John felt physically sick as he rushed up the stairs, Saron's mum was crying at the entrance to the ward. "John thank you for coming, I have something terrible to tell you, she has lost the baby, I am so sorry" John could feel himself welling up inside and his eyes becoming moist. Again, he was going to be robbed of being a dad. "Have you had any updates on Saron?" "Well apparently she has a punctured lung and a lot of internal bleeding but that's all they have told me" "What happened?" "She was coming back from the wholesalers and as

SERVED COLD

she came over Dilley Dale moor
she lost control of her car and you
know there are quite a few spar
holes, she went down one,
apparently the police officer said
the car had flipped over several
times hitting a tree on the way
down, the car is a total wreck,
they said she was lucky to be
alive, apparently some guy saw it
all and phoned for the police but
he had gone by the time the
emergency services had arrived.
They said he must have tried to
help her though so I don't know
if he had been drinking or
something like that so left before
the police and everyone came but
I think if she survives, that man
probably will be responsible for
saving her"

SERVED COLD

It was almost 4.30am when the Surgeon called John and her mum into a side room. "I'm Mr Lyons, I'm the surgeon looking after your daughter. I assume they told you we couldn't save the baby? A little girl if that is any consolation. Saron hasn't got a mark on her face or body, all the injuries are internal, she has a punctured lung, she also has what we call intracerebral bleeding which causes loss of use of all limbs, she has subdural bleeding outside the brain, this can be very serious. She has multiple rib fractures, I'm afraid the list goes on. She is in an induced coma just now but for how long at this stage I really can't say. Now if you will excuse me Saron needs me more than you, I suggest you go home and come back tomorrow when

SERVED COLD

hopefully she will be on the ward" Mr Lyon walked briskly away leaving John and Saron's mum looking stunned at what they had just heard. "Would you like me to take you home?" "No, I will stay here John, I know you have work so please come back after work, if there is a change I have your number and will call you." "Thank you" John didn't want to leave but he had no choice with the case at a critical stage. On the way to Bixton he felt shattered emotionally and physically with no sleep. He called Donna to let her know the situation. "If I can get some staff John I will get over there" "Ok, let me know if there are any updates"

DI Smarty was the first one to come to John's office. "Mate I am

SERVED COLD

really sorry to hear about Saron"
"It's not good Dave, we have lost
the baby as well" "Oh mate, I am
sorry, have you been at the
hospital all night?" "Yes why?"
"You look dreadful, go home and
get some sleep, I can watch over
this lot" "Think I might have to
mate, are you sure?" "John of
course I am, any updates I will
call you"

John got back and sat in the chair,
next thing he was fast asleep.
Around 2.00pm Dave Smarty
rang John, "Hi Mate, you ok?"
"Yeah, I feel a lot better for a few
hours rest" "Well it doesn't rain
but it pours. Just had the Post
Office on, the guy delivering the
mail to a Mr Yettin who lived at
Miller Mount Cottage, Dilley
Dale Moor said he noticed a light
on in the living room and

SERVED COLD

something moving so he took a look and it appears the guy has committed suicide, do you want to meet me there John?" "Ok mate I'll see you there" John quickly showered to freshen himself up then headed for Dilley Dale Moor. It felt a bit ironic that this was happening where Saron had her accident. There weren't a lot of houses on Dilley Dale Moor so John soon found Miller Mount Cottage, steered there by the blue flashing lights. Gammon entered the house, Di Smarty was waiting, he handed him a suicide note. "You need to read this John"

Gammon unfolded the note. It read.,

"Dear Mr Gammon

History may call me a serial killer but I have outlined the facts and

SERVED COLD

as I said once my revenge was complete, that was it.

Obviously I could not have my revenge on the perpetrator but I did on their descendants. My name is Mosha Yettin, I am a Jewish descendant. My mother, grandparents four uncles, four aunts and twelve cousins were all murdered in Auschwitz. My grandfather survived but he was a broken man, he told my father of the horrors they had to daily contend with and he named the scum that turned against their own people. Below are the people I murdered and why.

Number one: Ruth Weisner. I met Ruth at the meetings, she was oblivious like most of the victims to what their ancestors did. Her grandmother cleaned the poor

SERVED COLD

girls that were made to give their bodies to anybody the SS or the Kapo's who thought they deserved free sex in shed twenty-four, if the girls complained she would beat them. Their choice was do or die, some choice hey Mr Gammon?

Number two: Josef Guran, his grandfather was Herschel Sparks, another Kapo, he sent three of his own relatives to the gas chamber just to save his own skin.

Number three: James Sinclair, his father was Ezra Sully, an evil Kapo, the prisoners called him FAR SHARIR or EVIL RAT, my father said he would laugh if he beat somebody to death.

Number four: Maurice Gates, his father was Fritz Oogala, he was the only victim that accepted his

SERVED COLD

fate, he said before I killed him that a man must accept the sin of their father so he knew what Oogala had done.

Number five: Bernard Dyan, he wasn't actually number five but I have placed them in the order you found them Mr Gammon. I do regret his body was left to rot, he had paid his dues. His father was Frankel Hosentstie a German Jew and probably the cruellest Kapo, my father told me he delighted in degrading the prisoners, he would spit in their food well, if you could call it food, because he knew they had to eat it then he would walk away laughing.

Number six: Hendrik James and my biggest regret, his father was Remo Gunter, it wasn't until I overheard at the Jewish

SERVED COLD

Community what a fine man Remo Gunter was that I realised that my father had got this one wrong. Maybe it was the name as there were several Remo's in the camp. For the killing of Hendrik I will be eternally ashamed.

Number seven: Robin Lensky, his father was a Waffen SS and then SD officer, Paul Seeler. He was cruel with a capital C, he loved taking pictures father said of the girls in shed twenty-four after as many as twenty men had abused them. One poor girl refused to pose for him, she was probably losing her mind after being subjected to the pain and shame every day, my father said Seeler just calmly shot her then took a picture before laughing and walking away. My father hated him the most and he said he and

SERVED COLD

two other prisoners made a pact
that when their turn came to be
gassed they would jump him, take
his gun and shoot him. It never
happened, my father survived. It
wasn't until I discovered who
Robin Lensky was when he
confided in me the letter his
mother showed him, little did he
realise I now had the missing
piece of the jigsaw.

My work is now done and
revenge certainly is better served
cold as they say,

You may not like what I have
done but these people
masqueraded as Jewish survivors,
may they rot in hell"

On my way I think I may have
saved a beautiful young woman's
life, she had a car accident and
wasn't breathing. I revived her

SERVED COLD

and called the Emergency services but left as they arrived. Hopefully history will at least understand my crimes but also know I am a good man.

Mosha Yettin

"John you look puzzled ?" "Dave, he doesn't mention DS Yap or Myra Sinclair, why?" "Maybe he didn't kill them" "I'm certain he didn't, he did what he believed he had to do so we still have a killer at large. Look Dave, I need to get back to the hospital and Saron" "No problem, I'll sort out this end mate"

SERVED COLD

Chapter 12

John arrived at the hospital to be
told she was in a private ward in
the High Dependency Unit. There
were lots of pipes coming out of
Saron and she was still in a coma.
Hr mother was sat at her bedside
caressing her hand, "Hello John"
"What have they said?" "Very
little, all they have told me is if
she comes out of the coma it
could be weeks even months and
then she could be seriously ill for
the rest of her life, I'm afraid they
simply don't know" "I need to go
back to work, if there is any
change please let me know" "I
will John, I promise"

John felt bad but there was
nothing he could do for Saron
and the suicide note was bugging
him. He decided to go back to

SERVED COLD

Dilley Dale Moor and have a look around the house, just in case the full story wasn't being told by the suicide note.

He arrived at the house and one beat lad was at the scene. "I'm going to have a look around young man" "Ok sir" Downstairs there was nothing to suggest that this man was a killer but upstairs Gammon was surprised, he found a board a picture of all the men that were murdered, it looked like a day out at the sea-side, along-side of them was Abigail Harrop, no surprise there Gammon thought as the second victim had been her boyfriend. Gammon sat on the bed looking at the picture then realised that not only was Abigail in the picture but the killer was too!!

SERVED COLD

Gammon decided to call Abigail. Her phone rang and rang but no answer so he decided to go to her house. He arrived at Ash Lane Reservoir in Winksworth and Abigail's house but again no answer. Just then a lady walking a little Jack Russell was walking past. "Excuse me who are you?" "Oh sorry, I'm DI John Gammon, Bixton Police" and he showed her his warrant card. "I'm looking for Abigail Harrop have you seen her?" "No, she left in quite a hurry, she said she was going on holiday I know she was very upset about her friends' murders" "Friends?" "Yes, her and Mosha would quite often have barbecues in the summer with their Jewish friends, I think she was

SERVED COLD

wondering if she was next on the list because everyone of her friends were murdered and I heard her boyfriend Mosha had taken his life" "Mosha Yettin was her boyfriend?" "Well it was a bit messy, she lived with Josef but I think at these parties she kind of connected with Mosha, lovely man" "If I showed you pictures of the men would you be able to tell me if they were Abigail's friends?" "Of course, I may be almost eighty but I have good eyesight" she said proudly. Gammon reached in his pocket and pulled out the seaside picture. "Go left to right, who is that?" "Ruth, she made lovely sauces for the barbecues" "So that is Ruth Weisner, next one?" "That's Josef, I don't think he had a clue about Abigail and Mosha but I

SERVED COLD

caught them kissing, I never told anybody, I didn't want to upset Josef and the lovely barbecues we had" "Ok, next one?" "That's James, me and his wife were good friends, she would make trifles for the parties. The Sinclair's were great, such a shame what happened to them" "Next?" "Maurice, dear Maurice, I wish I had been thirty years younger, he was gorgeous even though he was in his mid -sixties. He would bring cherries, I love Cherries, do you Mr Gammon?" "Not really" "They are very good for treating gout" Oh, I will remember that"

"So, the next one?" "That's Bernard, very quiet man, hardly knew him to be honest" "Ok, next one?" "Hendrik, now there was a nice man, he would bring the

SERVED COLD

most succulent steaks to the barbecue. "That was Hendrik James?" "Yes, I used to always joke with him that his name was back to front, it should have been James Hendrik" and she smiled. "Ok, and this one?" "Robin Lensky, nice man, always seemed troubled to me though as if he was carrying the whole world on his shoulders and the front two are Mosha and Myra kneeling down" "Ok, thank you Mrs?" "Miss Sally Royston" "Oh, I'm sorry" "I no never married Mr Gammon" "Where do you live?" "Just up the road, it was Dilley Dale stables years ago but they've only got four fields now and a big shed which Abigail rented off me. She said she had arty work she did in there, I never went down there, my legs are not

that good on rough ground" "Ok
Miss Royston, thank you for your
help"

She carried on walking very slowly
down the road. Gammon was
pleased with the conversation but it
was now almost 5.40pm so he
decided to call at the Spinning
Jenny for a quick drink. On the way
he told PC Magic to arrange a
meeting in the incident room for
9.00am then he carried on to the
pub as he pulled into the car park
Saron's Mum called. "John they
said she is as comfortable as can be
expected, she is still in a coma, they
said I should bring some music in
to play to her they said that
sometimes works. To be honest it's
so long since she has been at home
I don't know what she likes and I
don't have a gadget to play
anything on." "Don't worry, I'll

SERVED COLD

bring you my I pad and set it up with her favourite songs. What time will you be at the hospital?" "Possibly 10.00am if that is ok John" "No problem, I will pop down and see you, she is a strong girl, she will get through this" "I know John, I'm just so sorry you lost the baby, I thought that would get you together again, I know she loves you very much"

John didn't know what to say, he just thanked her for the kind words. He got out of his car, it was quite a dreadful night as he walked down the steps to the back entrance of the Spinning Jenny, once inside he saw Phil Sterndale was sat at the bar. "Hey how are you Phil?" "Not bad John how about you? I hear you cracked the serial killer case" "News travels fast mate" "You know the local jungle drums

SERVED COLD

John!" and Phil laughed. "Out on your own?" "Yeah, Linda had a sewing class or something, sorry to hear about Saron, how is she?" "Not good, we are at the hospital every day, she is in a coma and they don't know how long for or what state she might be in when she eventually comes around" "We are all rooting for her John" "Appreciate that Phil" John had a couple of more beers then headed back home. He noticed three missed calls from Sheba but didn't return them, he somehow felt guilty with Saron at death's door. He arrived spot on time the next day for the meeting in the incident room. "Ok Wally, anything untoward about the suicide?" "No it had been meticulously carried out, no foul play, this man intended killing himself. I have had the

SERVED COLD

letter analysed by the lab against some other letters we had found in the house and it's definitely his hand writing so I believe we have the killer" There was a cheer from the team, Gammon stood up. "We are not celebrating yet, we still have to find the killer of Myra Sinclair and of course Ian. I have come to the conclusion that Mosha Yettin had an accomplice" "Who do you think it is sir" "Well DS Bass, I found a photograph in his bedroom which was taken at some seaside trip and all the people murdered were on there except Myra and Ian. One other person was on there and to be honest I don't want to believe it because she has helped me with the case" "Who is it?" "Abigail Harrop, she rents a shed at the old horse stables down a field, the old lady who owns the field never goes down to the large shed. I'm wondering if the killings and tattooing were done there so I want DI Smarty DI Milton and DS Bass to accompany me and let's go and do a search" The meeting broke up and they left for Dilley Dale Stables. Miss Royston was surprised to see Gammon again. "Miss Royston, after our conversation yesterday I got to thinking and I wondered if you would allow me and my colleagues to search the barn that Abigail Harrop rents from you?" "Well she doesn't pay me, I let Abigail use it that's all so legally I can go in anytime, correct Mr Gammon?" "Absolutely Miss Royston" "Ok, well here is the spare key, feel free"

SERVED COLD

John could see why Miss Royston at her age didn't go down the field, it was quite a hike from the house but when they got there Gammon noticed there was a road behind the barn so access was from the house but more importantly by the country road, Gammon undid the lock and they went inside. Switching on the light the horror hit them. There were pictures of all the previous tattoo holders in Auschwitz with names against them and the victims, it looked like Abigail had befriended these people then found out if any were related, if they were they were drugged and she tattooed them then Mosha killed them. There was so much incriminating evidence. Gammon could not believe it that Abigail was involved. "Sir look at this" "What you got Kate?" "She

definitely left in a hurry, she left a
memory stick, I just plugged it in
and its e mails she sent to Mosha
look"

"Mosha, James Sinclair's wife
gave DI Gammon a picture of her
husband's ancestor, I had no choice
but to kill the old bat once
Gammon pieced the puzzle
together. You killing DS Yap at
Ackbourne the other night wasn't a
plus for us in our quest, bloody
copper, if he hadn't have been
snooping you would not have had
to kill him. Now they are closing in
on us we need to get them all done
then get out of here back to Israel.
At least I will have avenged my
poor grandma for the use of her
body by those Kapo's who are the
lowest of the low and that
perverted Seeler's ancestor, make a
good job of him Mosha, I will start

SERVED COLD

making plans for our escape. We will be helped by our people so hold your nerve and we will be together in Israel very soon. I love you my darling xxx

"Get onto all the airports and ferries, let see if we can apprehend her and get Wally down here with the team Dave please. Look mate, I have to get over to the hospital"

"You get off John, I will sort this out" John realised it was now almost 1.00pm and Saron's mother would be waiting, he rushed to the hospital, she was sat crying.

"Where's Saron?" His heart sank.

To be continued ....

SERVED COLD

A big thank you as usual to Mandy Kiernan for the proof reading and to Martyn Wright for the Book Cover done to the usual high standard.

Thanks both of you

Colin J Galtrey.

Printed in Great Britain
by Amazon

41121635R00203